Cinder

Marie Sexton

Copyright

Copyright 2014, Marie Sexton

Editing by Sue Laybourn
Cover art by L.C. Chase
Formatting by Kelly Smith

http://mariesexton.net

EBooks are not transferable. All Rights are reserved. No part of this book may be used or reproduced in any manner without written permission, except in the case of brief quotations embodied in critical articles and reviews. The unauthorized reproduction or distribution of this copyrighted work is illegal. No part of this book may be scanned, uploaded or distributed via the Internet or any other means, electronic or print, without the author's permission.

This book is a work of fiction. The names, characters, places and incidents are products of the writer's imagination or have been used fictionally and are not to be construed as real. Any resemblance to persons, living or dead, actual events, locale or organizations is entirely coincidental.

Original publication date, February 3, 2012, by Silver Publishing.
2nd edition published by Marie Sexton, 2014
Paperback 2018

EBook ISBN: 978-0-9914153-2-8
Paperback ISBN: 978-0-9988501-5-3

1

Once upon a time there was a beautiful maiden who fell madly in love with a handsome young knight. They had a magical, whirlwind romance, and then the knight swept his lady off to a far-away land and married her.

But they did *not* live happily ever after.

Ten years to the day after their wedding, they were killed in a fire, leaving me, their only son, behind to be raised by my mother's twin sister. Aunt Cecile was recently widowed with twin daughters of her own. It was bad enough my mother had run off with a knight rather than marrying a proper gentleman, thereby leaving a black mark on the family name, but she had now left me with no money or inheritance of my own. Aunt Cecile already harbored a great deal of resentment. Being saddled with me didn't improve her disposition. And if I sometimes thought fate had been a bit unfair, it was a matter I chose not to dwell on.

The day I met the prince started like any other. I rose early to do chores—stoking the fire, collecting eggs, feeding the animals, and then helping our old cook Deidre prepare a late breakfast for the family. My cousins, Jessalyn and Penelope, were more agitated than normal.

"I'm telling you, mother," Penelope said, "the servants are all talking about it."

Jessalyn glanced pointedly in my direction and rolled her eyes. "Servants?" she said with obvious disdain. "What do they know?"

Cinder

"Sometimes, quite a bit," Aunt Cecile answered. "Servants hear things. They see things others don't." She turned to me. "Cinder, what have you heard?"

They rarely bothered to talk to me at all, unless it was to give me orders. Cecile's question brought me up short. They'd certainly never asked my opinion on anything. I cleared my throat. "Well, I heard the same things Penelope heard—that the prince is in town. But I also heard there's a group of diamond-hoarding dwarves living in the woods, and that the king from the next country over is burning every spinning wheel in his land because he's afraid of spindles, and that Bella's maid kissed a frog and it turned into a duke." I shrugged. "Servants gossip a lot. I don't believe most of what I hear."

"You see?" Jessalyn said to her sister. They were twins, but not quite identical. Both had long, beautiful dark hair and pleasing faces, but what was pretty on Penelope was ravishing on Jessalyn. Everything about her seemed to shine. Unfortunately, her personality didn't exactly match her lovely exterior. She sneered at me in disgust. "Nothing but lies and rumors."

But Aunt Cecile wasn't ready to dismiss it. "Who says the prince is here?" she asked me.

"Well, I heard it from Tomas who heard it from Anne, who heard it from Tabby. Tabby's maid heard it from her brother. He works at the stable at the inn down the road. *He* told her he talked to one of the prince's guard, and the guard told him—"

"That the prince is coming here to find a bride!" Penelope finished for me. She was practically bouncing in her seat from excitement.

"Right," I concluded. "That's what I heard."

Jessalyn eyed me with cold calculation, then turned to regard her sister and mother. She hated to be seen to agree with me on anything, but she also wasn't stupid. It was obvious she had nothing to gain by continuing to insult me and everything to gain by embracing the drama. She was clearly assessing the situation, trying to decide how to switch sides and make it seem as if she'd been in the right all along.

"Penny has a point," she said at last to her mother. "If the prince came here, he would have had to stay at the inn on his way, and Tabby's brother does work there. And if it's true the prince is coming here to find a bride, then we need to be prepared. You want us to make a good impression, don't you?"

Aunt Cecile smiled indulgently at her daughter. "Of course I do."

And so it was that Aunt Cecile bundled Jessalyn and Penelope into the carriage and headed for the seamstress to secure new dresses for them both.

"It'll take more than pretty dresses to get either of those two ninnies into the palace," Deidre said to me, once they'd gone. "Ugly girls!"

"They're not ugly, though," I said. "Jessalyn especially has a good chance of catching the prince's eye."

"Bah!" she spat. "He can have her. If all he wants is a pretty face, then he deserves to end up with a brat like Jess."

I suspected the prince would indeed be interested in more than a pretty face—specifically, graceful curves and swelling cleavage—but I chose not to share that with Deidre. "I'm going down to the river," I told her. "I'll catch us some fish for dinner."

"Don't forget to leave some for the witch." She told me that every time.

"I won't."

I set off through the woods with my pole over my shoulder. It was a beautiful fall day. Sun shone down through the branches, dappling the mossy ground. Birds sang in the trees. Chipmunks regarded me with suspicion as they scurried across my path. It felt unbelievably fortuitous to be

Cinder

granted a bit of free time on such a gorgeous morning. I whistled as I walked, a barely-remembered tune from my youth.

It felt good to be alive.

Midway to the river was a small clearing in the woods. It was a place I often sat when I had time to spare. Usually, it was empty save for wildlife, but not today. In the middle of the small meadow stood a man. He was about my age, tall and handsome. And he wore only one shoe. I rarely saw anybody in the woods, and it brought me up short.

"Good morning," he said as I stumbled to a halt.

"To you, as well," I managed to reply.

"Lovely day, isn't it?"

"It is."

"Say, watch out for Milton."

"Who?" I asked.

That very next instant, something massive slammed into me from behind, knocking me face first to the ground. An enormous weight on my back held me down. My first thought was that I was being robbed, except I had nothing for them to steal. My second thought was that Milton, whoever he was, had a breathing problem. He was panting heavily into my ear, his breath hot on the back of my neck.

"Milton!" the man scolded. "Let him go!"

The weight disappeared, and Milton, who turned out to be the biggest dog I'd ever seen, rushed panting and wiggling to his master's side. He probably weighed as much as I did. He had short hair and drooping jowls. In his mouth was a shoe.

"Sorry about that," the man said as he took his shoe from the dog. "He's still just a puppy."

"A puppy?" I said, as I got to my feet, brushing dirt and leaves and moss off the front of my shirt. "He's enormous."

"Well, yes. They're bred that way." He turned and threw his shoe toward the woods, and Milton ran gleefully after it.

"He's the best hunting dog in the kingdom. Or so they say."

"Who's 'they'?"

"My father's kennel master. They bred him and trained him. They say he could track a phantom stag to the far side of the world. Not that I've ever tested that theory."

"You don't believe them?"

"I believe them. I just don't care."

"Why not?"

"Hunting bores me. I ride along behind Milton while he does all the work, then I have to butcher the animal and haul its stinking corpse back to the palace so they can all gush about it and pretend I did something special." He shrugged. "Plenty of men who hunt because they have to. Let them have the deer. Milton and I prefer playing fetch."

I was hung up on one word. "Palace?" I asked. And then the magnitude of my stupidity caught up with me.

I dropped quickly to my knees, lowering my gaze to the ground. Here I was, facing the prince, and I'd been talking to him as if he were just another servant. "Your Highness, please forgive me. I didn't recognize you."

"Why would you have? We've never met."

"My behavior was inexcusable."

He laughed. "On the contrary. I wear no sign of my title, save my ring, which you could hardly see from all the way over there. We've never met before, which means you had no way of knowing who I was. Therefore, it seems to me your behavior is *entirely* excusable."

I risked raising my eyes. He was looking down at me with obvious exasperation.

He sighed. "For heaven's sake, get up!"

First I felt foolish for not having recognized him, and now he'd made me feel foolish for thinking I should have. I got to my feet again, brushing leaves from my knees. Milton returned the shoe, and the prince turned and threw it again toward the woods. He seemed to have forgotten I was there.

Cinder

I stood watching them play fetch, wondering what in the world I should do next. On one hand, I should not be talking to him, and if I continued to do so, I'd undoubtedly say something foolish. He was, after all, a prince, and I was nothing but a servant in my aunt's house. It was inappropriate for me to speak to him without being spoken to first. On the other hand, I couldn't leave without being excused.

I reached down and retrieved my fishing pole from the ground, where it had landed when Milton knocked me down. The movement seemed to catch his attention, and he turned to me. "Are you leaving?" he asked.

"Sire, with your permission—"

"Stop!" He sighed as he threw the shoe again for Milton. He shook his head. "I liked you much better when you thought I was nobody special."

That brought me up short. He'd liked me? My heart skipped a beat at the thought.

But now he didn't like me anymore.

"What's your name?" he asked.

"Cinder." Except that wasn't technically correct. Cinder was my surname, and it was what my aunt and cousins called me. Nobody called me by my first name. "Eldon."

He raised his eyebrows at me. "Well, which is it?"

"It's Eldon Cinder."

"It's wonderful to meet you, Eldon," he said. "I'm Augustus Alexandre Kornelius Xavier Redmond." He laughed. "But you know that now, don't you?"

"Yes, Sire."

"Don't call me 'sire.'"

"But—"

"My father calls me August. My mother calls me Alex. You can call me Xavier."

"That wouldn't be appropriate."

"Appropriate is boring." He turned to me again. "Where

are you going?"

"Fishing."

"Really?" he asked, suddenly alert and interested. He eyed the fishing rod I held. "With *that*?"

What kind of question was that? I looked at the pole, trying to see what about it was remarkable.

"You really catch fish with a stick?" he asked.

"It's a fishing pole."

"How does it work?"

I might have thought he was trying to play me for a fool, but his expression wasn't mocking. He seemed genuinely intrigued. "Haven't you ever fished before?"

"My father says fish are for peasants. He refuses to let it be served. But once, I sneaked down to the servant quarters, and they gave me some. It was delicious!"

I was trying to decide if I was offended by the peasant comment. He seemed oblivious. He eyed my rod again. "Do you stab them?"

"No! I put bait on the hook, and when a fish swallows the bait, I pull it out of the water."

"So you catch them one at a time?"

"How else would I do it?"

"I have no idea," he said, smiling. "I've never much thought about it." Milton came back again with the shoe, but instead of throwing it, the prince stared at me, his eyes bright and merry. "You're going there now?"

"Yes."

"Perfect," he said, pulling his shoe onto his bare foot. "Lead the way!"

And so I did.

It was strange, walking through the forest as I always did, carrying my fishing pole, but this time with a prince at my heels.

I glanced back to see if he was really there. He was staring up at the treetops, paying no attention at all to where he was going. If I'd done that, I would have tripped and fallen on my face. Apparently princes were granted a bit more natural grace.

Milton barked and frolicked around us, dashing ahead to scout the path, then running back to us as if to say, 'Hurry up, will you? I don't have all day!' Then he'd dart off again, howling and baying as if he was on the trail of some mighty prey.

The forest was silent in our wake. Even the trees seemed to be holding their breath, waiting for Milton and his two plodding humans to pass. I felt as if I should say something, but I had no idea what. How did one start a conversation with a prince?

"Why do you keep looking at me like that?"

I hadn't quite realized I was doing it until he called me on it, but he was right. I'd been staring at him as much as I was able with him following me. I shook my head. "This has to be the strangest thing that's ever happened to me."

"Going fishing?"

"Going fishing with you, yes."

"Are you saying I'm strange?"

I laughed. I couldn't help myself. "Well, you're the prince, and you're following a servant to go fishing. Does that seem normal to you?"

"I suppose not. But you're not exactly normal yourself, are you?"

"What makes you say that?"

"You know who I am, and yet you're not falling all over yourself in an attempt to curry some type of favor from me."

"Would you prefer that?"

"God, no. But that's how it usually works. Everybody wants something. Money, or a job for their father, or a marriage for their daughter." He smiled over at me. "Go ahead. Tell me what you'd ask for."

What would I ask for? I had to think about it. Certainly

money or a job outside of my aunt's house might have been nice, but it wasn't the desire that lurked in the deepest recesses of my heart. "Can you bring my parents back?" I asked.

"From where?"

"From death."

The smile faded from his face. "I'm afraid that's a bit beyond my abilities."

He seemed to be taking the request seriously, and I tried to laugh, although it came out flat. "I didn't really think you could."

"Did they die recently?"

I shook my head. "A long time ago. I was just a boy."

"I'm sorry."

We'd veered into something I didn't want to dwell on. It was definitely time to change the subject. I was relieved when Milton came bounding back, ears flapping and tongue lolling. His innocent doggy joy gave me a reason to laugh. "Are the rumors true?" I asked, as Milton turned and darted back into the woods. "Are you here to find a bride?"

"Is that what they're saying?"

"The town's abuzz."

"Bad news travels fast."

"So it *is* true?"

"I'm the prince, but not the Heir Confirmed. In order to be the true heir to the kingdom, I must be named crown prince."

"And to do that, you have to be married?"

"The law says I must take a bride by my next birthday."

"And when is that?"

"In two weeks."

"Cutting it a bit close, aren't you? What happens if you don't?"

"I'll be forced to renounce my crown, my title, and all claim to my inheritance."

"Ouch."

"No kidding."

"Why here? Seems like a long way to come to find a bride."

He glanced sheepishly my way. "I'd already rejected all the young ladies back home, so my father brought me to your township with the explicit order that I *would* find a wife."

"And here you are, hiding in the forest with your dog."

"I didn't say I intended to cooperate."

"You don't want to be the crown prince?"

He looked down at the forest floor, shoving his hands deep into his pockets. "I want very much to be my father's heir. I just don't want to take a bride."

I wasn't sure what to say to that, so I chose to say nothing at all. We reached the riverbank, and Milton, who bounced around us in glee.

"What about you?" Xavier asked. "Are you married?"

"No."

"Why not?"

Partly because I'd never desired women at all. I found men much more appealing, but I didn't want to tell him that. "I'm just a servant," I said. "Not even that, really. I'm not even paid a proper salary. I'm not exactly the most eligible bachelor around."

"It's funny, isn't it?" Xavier said. I turned to find him watching me, a spark of amusement in his eye as he scratched behind Milton's rather impressive ears.

"What?"

"We have opposite problems. Everybody wants to marry me."

"And that's bad?"

"The thing is, it has nothing to do with *me*, and everything to do with the crown. They don't even know me." He flashed me a mischievous grin. "I could be a lecherous, drunken louse, with base and criminal impulses, and still the fathers would be lined up down the lane, ready to sell their daughters to me like chattel."

"I never thought of it that way."

"I find the whole thing barbaric."

I thought of my cousins, off buying new dresses in hopes of catching the prince's eye. Deidre had been right—it would take more than a pretty face and a silk gown to secure their prize. I couldn't help but laugh. "And *are* you a lecherous, drunken louse?"

His laugh was loud, and he clapped me on the back. "Only on my good days."

His fascination with my fishing pole was short-lived, but he stayed with me as I fished. He sat on a rock, alternately playing fetch with Milton and whittling at a piece of wood he'd found on the ground. He never seemed to stop asking questions, and I found myself telling him about my parents, and Aunt Cecile, and my cousins.

"You told me you were a servant," he said. "But you're her nephew."

"She prefers not to be reminded of the fact." And truth be told, so did I. At one time, I had longed for her to be a mother to me, but those days were long past.

I stayed far longer than I should have. The sun was falling in the sky, and Deidre would be waiting for the fish.

"Must you go?" he asked as I gathered my things.

"I'm afraid so. My Aunt will have it in for me as it is."

"May I walk with you?"

I was struck once again by the absurdity of being asked such a question by the prince, as if he needed my permission. "Of course. I could invite you back to the house for some fish. I'm sure my aunt would be happy to have you—"

"Dinner with the marriageable cousins?" he joked. "I'd rather not. Besides, Milton has terrible table manners."

I laughed, mostly out of relief. I was glad he'd declined

Cinder

the invitation. He would have been at the dining room table with the family, while I served them. He knew my place in their household, but the idea of having him witness it was too painful to bear. My aunt would go to great lengths to humiliate me. Watching Jessalyn and Penelope fawn over him would only make it worse. As it was now, he was a secret—a wonderful, joyous secret belonging only to me. The last thing in the world I wanted to do was share him.

"This isn't the way we came," he said as he followed me through the woods. "I hope you're not following Milton."

Milton had darted ahead of us again, seemingly trying to sniff every tree he saw. "I have a stop to make first."

"Where?"

"There's an old lady who lives here. I leave fish for her."

He didn't say anything else, just followed along behind as I made my way to the witch's cave.

"What kind of person lives in a cave?" he asked, as I lay the fish on the flat stone by the door.

I shrugged. "They say she's a witch. She can do magic."

He waved his hand at me dismissively. "I don't believe in magic." He peered into the mouth of the cave, but there was only darkness. Milton sniffed at the entryway, but seemed unwilling to venture inside.

"They say she can turn pumpkins into carriages and mice into horses."

He frowned at me. "That doesn't seem very useful."

I hadn't really ever thought about it much. What was the point of that kind of magic? "I suppose she could sell the horses."

"Then why don't you leave her mice? And why does she live in a cave?"

"I don't know," I said, trying not to be annoyed. He was a prince, after all, and his questions were valid, even if they did make me feel silly.

"Have you ever seen her?" he asked.

"No."

"How do you know she exists?"

"The fish I leave are always gone."

"You're probably keeping a big bear fat and happy."

I shrugged, feeling foolish. Deidre had taught me to always leave an offering for the witch. It seemed harmless enough, but now I regretted having let him see me do it.

"I've upset you," he said.

"No." Although I wasn't sure if it was true or not.

He watched me thoughtfully for a moment, then pulled something out of his pocket. He placed it on top of the fish. It was a small carving—the one he'd been working on as I fished. It was a dog, rough and inelegant, but clearly modeled on Milton. "Maybe the bear likes knick-knacks, too."

It wasn't really for the witch. It was for me. It was a peace offering, and I accepted it with a smile.

He continued to follow me as we left the witch's cave behind, eventually arriving in the clearing where we'd first met. I turned to face him, feeling awkward. He was tall and regal, and I wondered how I could ever have looked at him and not seen his nobility. Even with Milton panting at his feet, he practically radiated power. "I feel like I should bow or something."

He rolled his eyes. "Please don't."

I couldn't just say goodbye and walk away. That felt entirely wrong. Instead, I extended my hand to him. "It was a very great honor to meet you."

He smiled at me, reaching out to shake my hand. His fingers were strong and warm. "The honor was mine. Thank you for teaching me to fish."

"You're welcome, Sire." His eyebrows lowered, his smile turning into a glare, and I quickly amended, "Xavier."

I wanted to stay longer. I wanted an excuse to touch him again. I wanted this glorious, magical day to go on forever. But I had no way to make time stand still.

Reluctantly, I turned to leave. I was just entering the trees when he called out to me.

"Will you come again tomorrow?"

I turned to face him, although he was halfway across the clearing. "I'm not sure if I can."

"I am the prince, you know," he said. "I could command you to come."

I couldn't tell if he was serious or teasing. "I would have to tell my aunt. Is that what you want?"

"No." His gaze dropped to the ground. "I suppose I hadn't thought of that."

He seemed genuinely disappointed. The thought of it made my mouth dry. It caused a stir of butterflies in my stomach, and a rush of joy inside my chest.

Maybe. If I rose early. If I hurried through my chores. "I'll try to get away after serving lunch," I said.

His gaze met mine, and his smile was bright and gorgeous and unbelievably infectious. "I'll be waiting."

Aunt Cecile had let the other maids go years before, in order to save money. At first, my cousins had railed at the unfairness of being required to dress themselves. It wasn't long before any modesty they'd ever felt in my presence was overcome by a need to have somebody lace their corsets and brush their hair. Somehow over the years, I'd become embarrassingly adept at it.

My cousins knew the prince was in town, and because they seemed to feel there was a chance they might see him at the market (and I dared not tell them otherwise) I was required to spend extra time the next day on their thick, dark tresses. It was two hours past lunch when I finally managed to get away. I made my way through the woods with my heart lodged tight in my throat.

I felt silly. He was a prince, and I was a servant. Did I truly expect to find him waiting for me in the meadow like some heartsick lover? Did I really believe he had no better way to spend his time?

It was with a mixed sense of anticipation and dread that I neared the clearing, my fishing pole clutched firmly in my sweaty hand. I found him there, waiting, just as he'd promised. He was sitting on a fallen log in the middle of the clearing, alternately throwing his shoe for Milton and carving at a piece of wood. Milton nearly knocked me over in his excitement and Xavier smiled broadly at me as he stood, tucking the piece of wood into his pocket.

"You're here!" he said, spreading his arms as if to embrace me.

"Yes, Sire." I tried to sound respectful, as I felt I should, but it was hard with such an enormous grin taking over my face.

He scowled good-naturedly at me. "Don't call me 'sire.'" He eyed my pole. "Fishing again?"

"It gives me a reason to be gone." Otherwise, they'd wonder where I was all day. They'd come up with other chores for me to do.

Xavier retrieved his slightly-squished boot from Milton's mouth. "I suppose I either have to reveal myself to your marriageable cousins or make peace with the fish."

I smiled. "I believe that's correct, Sire."

"The fishes it is, then!" he said, pulling on his boot. He glanced over his shoulder at me as he turned toward the river. "And stop calling me 'sire!'"

⊗⊗⊗

And so it was that my friendship with the prince became the center of my life, for a few short days, at least. Each afternoon, I managed to spend a few glorious hours in his presence. He'd meet me in the clearing, and he'd sit with me as I fished. Afterward, I'd leave two fish for the witch, and Xavier would leave whatever he'd carved that day—one day a fox, the next day a kitten, the third day an owl. Then he would follow me to the edge of the clearing and ask, "Will you come again tomorrow?"

Of course I would. I would have moved heaven and earth to see him each and every day. Still, his presence was not without consequence.

My cousins were cranky and sullen. New dresses, powders and perfumes, plus hours of grooming in hopes of catching Xavier's eye, and yet it seemed the prince had barely been seen by anyone, in or out of the palace. He wasn't at the theatre. He wasn't at the shops. He wasn't even in the library, and Jessalyn bemoaned an entire two hours spent checking the aisles, finding nothing but moths and some dusty old books.

Aunt Cecile oversaw the housework with a newfound zeal. "What if the prince comes to call?" she asked at least once a day. "Will you have him find us in squalor?" Some days, it was all I could do not to blurt out that the prince had no intention of ever visiting her home. He'd made it quite clear he intended to stay far away from my "marriageable cousins."

Not surprisingly, my attention to my chores became scattered at best. My sudden distraction did not go unnoticed. Aunt Cecile remarked at dinner that the glasses still had lipstick marks from the day before. Penelope complained her laundry had been washed, but not put away. Jessalyn noted the fireplaces hadn't been swept in days.

All three of them were getting rather tired of eating fish.

I ignored them all. The only thing I cared about was spending as much time with Xavier as I could. I stayed a bit longer with him each day. I knew I was asking for trouble and yet I couldn't seem to help myself. He was somehow invincible—a force of nature I couldn't stand against. A flood that carried me with or without my consent. If he beckoned, I felt compelled to follow. I was light as a feather, and he was the wind.

It wasn't because he was the prince. At least, that wasn't the *only* reason. Certainly having the attention of somebody so important was flattering, but that wasn't why I hurried to the meadow each day to meet him. The real reason was far simpler. It was the fact that he waited for me. He smiled at me. He asked about my day. He listened when I talked. He laughed at my jokes. He asked nothing of me, except for the apparent pleasure of my company. He never commented on my low social standing, or my worn and tattered clothes. He never mentioned the calluses on my fingers, or the ashes in my hair, or the soot that stained my hands. And yet, he listened to me. He met my eyes when I talked. He spoke to me as an equal. He treated me as a friend.

He saw *me*, in a way nobody else in the world did. I was real to him. I mattered.

It was the most amazing gift I'd ever been given.

We had fun together, although we rarely did more than fish and talk while playing fetch with Milton. I looked forward to it every day. Every minute I was not in in his presence I spent thinking of when I'd see him again.

On the fourth day, though, I knew something was wrong. He wasn't his normal, jovial self. He sat on his usual rock next to the river, fidgeting with the ring on his finger, seemingly oblivious to everything around him. Milton had long since given up on fetch. He'd run off into the woods to find his own doggy adventure.

I waited for him to snap out of it, and when he didn't, I spent a long time debating whether I should ask what was bothering him. He was my friend—of course I should ask. But he was also the prince. It was none of my business.

"You seem upset today," I said at last. I tossed my line

in the water and turned to watch him closely for signs I'd overstepped my bounds.

He didn't seem bothered by my words. He stared at his hands, fiddling with his signet ring. "My father's quite cross with me, you know."

"Why is that?"

"All this time, he thought I'd been out courting a potential bride."

"And he found out otherwise?"

He continued to twist the ring on his finger. The ring symbolized his status as the prince. To him, it probably underscored the fact that he was not the crown prince. "I have something to tell you." His tone was so somber, somehow foreboding. "My father has taken matters into his own hands."

"He's chosen a bride for you?"

"No." He shook his head, looking up at me at last. "Not yet, at least."

"Then what?"

He smiled, although not his normal, bright smile. He seemed sad. "I'm sure your marriageable cousins will tell you all about it when you get home."

My cousins?

"Will you come to the clearing tomorrow, Eldon?"

"I'll try, of course, but—"

"Can you come earlier in the day?"

That would prove difficult. My aunt and cousins were already cross with me. "I don't know if I can."

"The thing is…." He hesitated, and I was surprised to see a slow blush creeping up his cheeks. "Tomorrow will be the last day I'll have with you."

Was it possible my heart stopped beating? The world seemed to spin around me. I felt sick.

Of course I'd known he wouldn't be around forever, but somehow, I'd let myself forget just how little time I might have with him.

One more day?

It wasn't enough. It would never be enough.

I had to swallow hard against a knot in my throat. I became aware of my fishing pole in my hand, the line being dragged away in the river as I stood there. It felt symbolic. I was as insignificant as my lure, and Xavier was the current. He'd carried me for a while, but I could only go as far as my line allowed. He'd move on—down the hill, around the bend, toward the falling sun—and I'd still be here, on the bank of the river.

Only now, I'd be alone.

"Eldon?"

I had to force myself to speak. "Yes?" My voice came out a whisper. He probably couldn't even hear me over the sound of the rushing water.

"I won't be able to stay late tomorrow, but I'd really like to see you before I go."

"I'll be here."

⬥

My cousins were indeed buzzing with news when I arrived home. The king was throwing a ball.

It wasn't like any other ball I'd ever heard of. Every maiden in the township was invited, but none of the men. Each girl was guaranteed one dance with the prince, and his bride would be chosen that evening. After that, the royal family and the princess-to-be would head back to the capital, and I'd never see him again.

I rose early the next day. I rushed about in a frantic effort to finish my chores so I could meet him, if only for a few minutes. But my cousins had other plans.

There was only one seamstress in town, and she'd been barraged by frantic women in need of dresses for the ball. My

Cinder

cousins didn't take priority. They knew they had to make do with what they had. Penelope bore it well, but Jessalyn was in a rage. We rushed about all day, trying to find something she approved of. We raided Aunt Cecile's closet, and called on the married woman next door as well. Deidre did most of the sewing, but it seemed she constantly needed my help. Ruffles and petticoats were removed and re-sewn, necklines lowered, sleeves shortened. I was sent to town three different times, once for a sash, once for gloves, and a third time for earrings in an exact shade of blue. I felt each second tick by. The sand through the hourglass mirrored my hope as it drained away.

I'd never make it in time.

After that, I had to do their hair. Long, loose waves for Penelope, then Jessalyn's up in an artful tangle of curls. I was a bit more forceful than usual as I strapped them into their corsets. Luckily, they were desperate enough to have tiny waists. They didn't object. And finally, they were bundled into our carriage and sent on their way.

At last, I was free.

I rushed through the forest. How long might he have stayed? Would I have a few minutes? The sun was already dipping low behind the tops of the wind-blown trees.

Just let me say goodbye.

I stumbled into the clearing at last, and whatever hope I'd had left died inside my chest.

It was empty.

"Xavier?" I called. Maybe he had only just left. Maybe he'd hear me and come back. But there was no answer.

With a heavy heart, I made my way to the center of the clearing and the fallen log he always sat on as he waited. Sitting on top of it was a gift. It was one of his carvings. The others I'd seen had been rough—recognizable, but done halfheartedly as we talked. This one, though, he'd clearly spent time on. It was a fish. Only a fish, no longer than my little finger, and yet it was beautiful. Its body curved, as if it were leaping from the rapids. Its tail was as delicate as lace. Its tiny scales were perfect.

I cupped it in my hands, and I let my tears fall. There was nobody to see me. There was nobody to know. I sank to the ground, curled against the log, and I cried.

He was my only friend, and he was gone.

I cried as the sun finally sank below the horizon. I cried until I fell asleep.

I woke to the low drone of cicadas. The western edge of the sky was still brushed with pink. The moon was beginning to rise. I hadn't been asleep long.

It took me a moment to take stock. I was in the clearing. Xavier was gone.

Behind me, somebody cleared their throat.

I turned around, hoping to see the prince. Instead, I found a woman sitting on the fallen log. Her body was covered in a gray shroud that was little more than a rag. I'd never seen her, but there was only person she could be: the witch.

"He waited a long time," she said. Her voice was scratchy and harsh, as if she smoked incessantly, although I saw no pipe in her hands. "He paced and fretted, but at last he went away."

She was hard to look at. Or, more specifically, she was hard to see. It was as if my eyes refused to focus on her. One minute, she seemed young as a maid. The next, she was older than Deidre. In the span of a few seconds, she seemed to be anywhere from twenty to ancient. Her hair, too, changed from one moment to the next, sometimes appearing blond and brilliant, at others gray and ratted. It might have been a dream, but the dampness of the ground I sat on and the kink in my neck told me otherwise.

"No fish for me today, boy?"

I cleared my throat and made myself speak. "No."

She laughed. Her voice may have been rough, but her laugh was melodic. Her voice spoke of age, but her laughter of youth. "I was growing weary of it anyway."

I glanced down at the wooden fish in my hand. I stroked its arching back. "I think I'm done fishing for a while." I wasn't sure I could bear to go without Xavier to keep me company.

"And what about that trinket you hold? I'd like to have it. I was looking forward to adding to my collection."

I closed my hand around protectively around the carving. "This one is for me."

"What's it worth to you?"

"It's all I have of him," I said, my voice quiet. "Please don't take it from me."

"What if I could give you something better in exchange?"

"You can't."

"Ah, so little faith." Her tone was chiding, but her eyes were kind. She smiled at me. At the moment, she seemed to be a woman just past the bloom of her youth, still regal and beautiful, but with the wisdom of accumulated years. "Tell me, young Eldon, what would you ask of me?"

Her words reminded me of Xavier and the day we'd met. I remembered so clearly the way he'd smiled at me as he'd said the words. *Go on. Tell me what you'd ask for.*

Back then, I had asked for my parents, but that wasn't the desire that now ruled my heart. "I'd ask to see him one more time."

"Just to see him?" she asked. "Would catching a glimpse of him be enough?"

I shook my head, looking again at the wooden fish tucked into my hand. "To speak to him," I said. "To say goodbye."

"Most people want the world. Most would ask for wealth, or true love. Any girl in the kingdom right now would ask to be his bride."

Of course they would, but I wasn't one of them. I was just a servant who'd gone fishing on the right day and been befriended by a prince. I'd already had more of him than I could ever have hoped.

"I only want to say goodbye."

She was silent. When I glanced up at her, she'd changed again. She was older now, although still not *old*—a middle-aged widow with a touch of gray in her hair and laugh lines around her eyes. "Would you like to go to the ball?"

"Only women are allowed in."

"Minor detail," she said. "Would you like to go?"

I thought about what she was hinting at. Would she sneak me in as a servant or a coachman? "Would I be able to see him? To speak with him?"

"Every maiden is guaranteed a dance."

"Every *maiden*?" The full impact of what she was implying finally hit me. The thought was both exhilarating and terrifying. "You'd make me a woman?"

"Is there any other way?"

Whether there was or not, I didn't know, but I knew I had no desire to be female.

"Don't worry," she said, as if reading my mind. "The spell will only last one night."

One night. One spell. One dance. And in exchange? I thought of the wooden fish clutched tight in my hand.

"Deal."

She held her hand out for the fish. I handed it over, telling myself it would be worth it.

I *hoped* it would be worth it.

"Give me your hands," she said.

I did as instructed. Her fingers on mine were dry and cool. Her hands felt fragile.

"Brace yourself," she said.

"Will it hurt?"

She smiled. "No. But you may find it disconcerting."

And then, she cast her spell.

I wasn't sure what I expected. Magic wands and chanting? Maybe a song and a shower of stars? The witch's spell included none of that. She closed her eyes. She continued to hold my hands. Her lips moved, but no sound emerged. She swayed a bit on her feet.

It started as a warm, tingling sensation in my fingertips and spread quickly up to my wrists. I gaped in surprise at what was left in its wake.

I now had the small, soft hands of a woman.

The warmth continued up my arms. My wrists became thin and delicate. The hair on my forearms seemed to withdraw into my flesh. My skin became smooth and pale.

The magic reached my torso and spread up my neck and down my spine. My shoulders narrowed. There was a tightening in my scalp, as if somebody were gently pulling my hair. My facial structure shifted, my ribcage shrank, my hips widened. The strangest sensation of all came next—the feeling of my center of gravity falling from somewhere above my navel to a spot between my hipbones. It was as if the ground had suddenly risen up to meet me, and yet, I also felt taller. I looked at the witch, who was still swaying with her eyes closed. She was still the same height in relation to me. I hadn't actually grown at all.

Along with the changes to my body came a change to my attire. My worn and tattered clothes were gone. The tightness of a well-laced corset constricted my ribcage, limiting my air. I now wore a flowing, satin gown. It was light green with a long, heavy skirt and a plunging neckline. I blushed as I looked down at the cleavage it revealed.

My cleavage!

I was shaken by a sudden sense of vertigo. I closed my

eyes and attempted to take a deep breath to calm myself, but the corset prevented me from getting the oxygen my brain screamed for. The witch's grip on my hands tightened. I opened my eyes. My vision seemed a bit spotty, but I could see her, watching me. She appeared to be older now, her face drawn and wrinkled.

"It's done," she said.

I sat down on the log and took several slow breaths. I couldn't breathe deep, but I forced myself to inhale and exhale until my vision cleared.

"How long will it last?" I asked.

"Until just before dawn."

It was only now just past sunset. I had plenty of time.

I took stock of myself. Now that the magic had finished, this body didn't feel so different from my own. The most notable difference was the tightness of the corset and the itchiness of the lace petticoats underneath my dress. I now had long, chestnut hair. Strands of it tickled my bare shoulders.

"You look like your mother," she said.

"Really?" I barely remembered my mother's face. I wished I had a mirror. I instinctively reached up to touch my face as if that would allow me to see her. My cheek was definitely not my own. It was smooth, with no hint of stubble.

"Don't let your aunt see you. Anybody else will likely mistake you for your cousins, but your aunt will think she's seen a ghost."

Of course. I hadn't thought of that. Aunt Cecile and my mother had been twins. And now her girls were twins, and I apparently resembled them. "What about Jessalyn and Penelope?"

She laughed and shook her head. "Their mother is too far past her youth for them to see your resemblance to her, and they're too caught up in themselves to notice your

Cinder

resemblance to them."

It was strange, knowing I wore my mother's body. Somehow comforting and disturbing, all at the same time. I looked down at my hands. I had long, delicate fingers. I wiggled my toes. There was something strange about my feet. I lifted my skirt a bit to peek down.

My clothes had changed, but not my shoes. I still wore my worn work boots, except now they were two sizes too big.

"Oh," the witch said in surprise. "I forgot the shoes."

I pulled my feet out of my boots and examined them. The shape of my toes was familiar, and yet the daintiness of my bones was not. My heel was narrower, and the gentle curve of my ankle was decidedly not masculine.

I was so busy examining my feet, I didn't see the shoes until she held them out to me. They were like no shoes I'd ever seen. They had two-inch heels, and the rest of them seemed to be made of nothing but thin straps of delicate lace. I was sure as soon as I took a step in them, they'd fall apart. They seemed entirely too small, but when I slid my foot inside of them, I found they fit perfectly.

"Stand up," she said.

I did, although I wobbled. The heels weren't outrageously high, but they were certainly higher than any I'd ever tried to walk in. They seemed determined to sink into the soft ground. It was hard to balance. I had to put my weight on the balls of my feet, which meant thrusting my shoulders back. All in all, it was anything but graceful.

The witch watched me, her lips pursing into a thoughtful frown. The gentle wrinkles around her eyes seemed to deepen.

When I finally had my balance, she said, "Let's see you walk."

The first few steps felt ridiculously clumsy, but after that, I felt I had the hang of it: shoulders back, weight on the balls of my feet, trying to keep my torso rigid and still so as not to lose my balance. I thought I was doing well until I heard her groan.

"What's wrong?" I asked, turning toward her.

"You look like a great lumbering oaf. Is that the best you can do?"

"It's not every day somebody turns me into a woman, you know."

"Plodding, clumsy men," she said in exasperation. "You'll be the laughing stock of the ball."

"It's not my fault!"

She shook her head and sighed. "This will take more magic than I thought."

I thought of the fish Xavier had left for me, now tucked somewhere inside her robes. "I have nothing else to give you."

"I'll fix it," she said. "Leaving you this way would be a waste of a perfectly good spell."

She took my hands, and once again, the magic spread up my arms and over my body. This time, there was no visible change, but there was a definite shift inside my body. I couldn't have said what it was exactly—just a subtle change in my posture, as if I were settling into familiar chair.

"Now let me see you walk."

It was the strangest thing I'd ever experienced. It was like moving though water, except of course there was only air. My brain would tell my body what to do, but somewhere between it and my limbs, something intercepted the message. Something translated the signals into a new language. When I moved, there was a gentle resistance against my limbs which seemed to smooth my movements. There was a new knowledge seated somewhere in my subconscious which told me to put my shoulders back, to arch the small of my back a bit, to let my hips move as I walked in order to accommodate my lower center of gravity.

Cinder

This time I felt graceful. Even having to adjust for the soft forest floor, I was able to walk the length of the meadow and back without stumbling.

"It's amazing!" I said, feeling excited and giddy. The witch's expression was solemn.

"This spell is more complicated. It won't last as long."

"How long?"

She pulled a watch on a thin silver chain out of her pocket and checked it. "You'll have until midnight."

Midnight.

Suddenly my enchanted evening had been reduced to only a few short hours. What had felt like hope now became something sad and ominous. "That's not much time," I said.

"It's not," she admitted. "I suggest you get going."

The horse cart and rickshaw drivers were out in force, happy to convey anxious young women to the ball in exchange for a few coins. The witch was kind enough to provide me with fare, and in no time at all, I found myself climbing the stairs to the castle.

I was a mess of nervous energy. My palms were embarrassingly sweaty. My heart beat a wild staccato inside my chest as I made my way to the ballroom. What would I say to him when I saw him?

As it turned out, I had plenty of time to ponder the question. A guard ushered me into a room full of women. A steward at the door handed me a small wooden chit with a number on it. "We'll call you when it's your turn," he told me. "After your dance, you can go home, or you can wait in the parlor with the rest."

I eyed the women. Each held a similar chit in her hand. It was disconcertingly like waiting my turn to buy bread at the bakery, except that everyone here was decidedly overdressed. I found an empty seat and settled in.

Some women paced. Some sat quiet and stoic. Some chatted idly with friends. A few were obviously summing up their competition. I spotted my cousins on the opposite side of the room. Penelope sat nervously chewing her cuticles. Jessalyn stood at a mirror, fussing with her hair. Neither of them noticed me.

Jessalyn's number was called next, but she quickly snatched Penelope's chit away and shoved her own into her sister's hand. "You go first," she said. "That way you won't have to sit here worrying any longer."

I knew that wasn't the real reason she wanted Penny to go first. Jess wanted to be able to upstage her sister. Still, Penny didn't argue. She went into the ballroom like a criminal marching to trial. Only a few minutes later, Jessalyn's number was called. I relaxed significantly once they were gone.

More women came in behind me. More left as their numbers were called. The seconds ticked by, and I began to worry I'd have to leave before my turn came. But at last, twenty minutes before the clock was to strike twelve, I found myself walking through the ballroom door.

The ballroom was large, lit with what must have been hundreds of candles. A group of musicians sat in the corner, silent at the moment. Opposite me was another door. My predecessor was just disappearing through it into what must have been the parlor. The prince stood near a buffet table, drinking a glass of champagne. His back was to me.

"X—" I cut myself short, realizing I'd been about to say his name. I corrected quickly and said, "Excellency?" instead.

He didn't turn to face with me. "I'll be with you in a moment."

I approached slowly, moving as quietly as I could in the ridiculous shoes. I didn't want to disturb him, but I didn't want to stand on the other side of the room, either.

Cinder

As I came nearer to the buffet, I saw it was covered with finger foods and refreshments. They appeared to have barely been touched.

"Not hungry tonight?" I asked.

He sighed and turned to look at me. His eyes were guarded and wary. "My father promised each maiden a dance, not dinner."

It amused me that he would meet his father's demands, and yet go not one step further. "I see."

He gestured over his shoulder at the door the last woman had left through. "There's quite a feast laid out in there, from what I hear, so the ladies don't go hungry as they await my decision."

I pictured another room full of women, much like the one I'd just left. Some would be nervous, some hopeful, some full of resentment. Some would undoubtedly be on their fourth or fifth glass of champagne.

"It sounds wonderful," I said.

He didn't seem to notice the hint of sarcasm in my voice. He looked me up and down with unabashed curiosity. "You look lovely," he said.

"Thank you, Sire. You look…." My words trailed away as I tried to decide how to end my sentence. Every other time I'd seen him, he'd been dressed casually, in clothes that were obviously of the highest quality, and yet designed for daily wear. This evening, he wore something that resembled a uniform. It was royal blue with stiff gold braids on the shoulders and across his chest. Its cut was tight and severe. He was as gorgeous as ever, but he didn't seem at ease.

I still hadn't finished my sentence, and he raised his eyebrows at me. "Charming?" he prompted. "Dashing? Handsome?" He wasn't digging for a compliment. His tone was teasing, and I knew he's probably been told all of those things this evening several times over.

"Uncomfortable," I said.

He laughed. The sound was short, but loud and genuine. "Indeed," he said. "I have renewed sympathy for you women and your corsets."

"You have *no* idea," I muttered under my breath, resisting the urge to tug on the one that bound my ribcage.

"Pardon?"

I decided it was best not to repeat myself. Instead, I gestured to the glass of champagne in his hand. "Do you intend to offer me a drink?"

He smiled. "No, I don't. Do you intend to curtsy like a proper lady?"

Of course I should have done it as soon as he'd turned to face me, but I hadn't thought of it. He was teasing though, not chastising, and I said, "No, I don't."

That made him laugh again. He turned and poured another glass of champagne. He held it out to me. "Happy now?"

I couldn't help but smile. I curtsied as I took the glass, a movement that was somehow unbelievably natural to this body I wore. "Thank you, Sire." My hand trembled as I raised the glass to my lips.

The champagne was unlike anything I'd ever tasted—sweet and bright and bubbly. It was better than anything my aunt ever had in her house. It tasted like morning sunlight. I should have sipped it, but it was too delicious, and I had too little time. I gulped it down all at once, and when I lowered the glass, I found him looking at me with obvious amusement.

"More?" he asked.

I felt myself blush. I didn't often drink. I imagined I could already feel the alcohol flowing through my blood, making me reckless and giddy. I put the empty glass down on the table. "I'm sure a second glass would be unwise."

He held his hand out to me. "Then I suppose this is when I ask you to dance."

Standing there talking to him had been easy, but reaching out to take his hand required every ounce of willpower I had. It felt like something I'd never come back from. His fingers were warm against mine. He pulled me toward him, and as he did, the musicians in the corner began to play.

I'd worried a bit about the dancing, but the witch's spell worked perfectly. I fell easily into step with him. It was strange and magical and amazing. My body moved in a way that was completely unfamiliar to me. It knew which way to step, even if I didn't. I didn't examine this new-found grace too closely for fear focusing on it would ruin the spell.

"You dance beautifully," he said after the first few steps.

"I don't really. It's the magic."

The words were out of my mouth before I had time to think better of them. His eyes widened in surprised amusement. "I don't believe in magic."

"Or course not. I only meant, I'm normally a bit clumsy. It's a miracle I haven't stomped all over your toes, or tripped over my own feet."

"Yes. Well, this is my eighteenth dance of the evening, so I guess we both have good reason to keep the steps simple."

Eighteen dances so far. I thought about the room full of women I'd just left. "There are at least another dozen girls behind me."

He sighed. "I'll be dead on my feet by morning."

"We could ditch the ball and go fishing."

He stopped mid-step, causing me to run into his chest. "You fish?"

I felt myself blush. Why had I said something so stupid? "I shouldn't have said that."

"On the contrary, it's a wonderful idea, except my father would have me drawn and quartered."

"An execution would put a real damper on the evening."

He laughed. "It would indeed."

He put his arm around me again, and we resumed dancing. It was wonderful, being so close to him, letting him guide me in slow circles around the dance floor. He was a force of nature, carrying me somewhere. I didn't know where I'd end up, and I didn't care.

He stared at me as we danced, as if studying me. It might have made me nervous, but I was too happy to mind much. His obvious scrutiny gave me an excuse to look back. I wanted to memorize every angle of his face, so I'd never forget.

"Have we met before?" he asked.

"No."

"You seem very familiar."

"You must be thinking of somebody else—"

"I don't think so. It's something about your eyes."

My heart jumped at his words, partly from joy, partly from an irrational fear he'd guess my true identity. "You must be confusing me with one of the women you danced with earlier."

"I suppose," he said, although it was clear he wasn't convinced.

"So many women, so little light. I'm sure we all begin to look the same."

"Some more than others." He lowered his voice and whispered, as if he were sharing a great secret, "Some manage to stand out."

His words pleased me, and I found myself smiling. "I'm glad I can liven up your dull evening. It must be so hard, spending the hours surrounded by beautiful, fawning women."

He laughed. "Now you're just being cruel."

"And you're being a tease."

He shook his head. There was amusement in his eyes, but something else, too. "You puzzle me," he said.

Cinder

"Why is that?"

"You're not like any of the other girls."

His words alarmed me a bit. I obviously wasn't playing my part well. "What do you mean?"

"They've all fallen into one of three categories. One: they spend the entire dance telling me how handsome and charming I am. Two: they find me terrifying, and can't even meet my eyes, let alone talk to me. Three: they spend every second of our time together telling me what a wonderful wife they'd be."

"Well, I think you're too charming and handsome to be terrifying, but I'm quite sure I'd make a terrible wife."

"Why do you say that?"

The question made me laugh out loud. If only he knew the truth. "There are too many reasons to list."

He shook his head again. "Definitely not like the other girls."

"I'll try to be more like them, if it will please you. Which of those three options would you prefer? I think I can pull off either of the first two, but the third might be beyond my abilities."

"No," he said. We'd been teasing, but suddenly he seemed serious. "I very much prefer you this way."

I felt myself blush. I could no longer look him in the eye. I found myself studying the gold braid at his throat. I had no idea what to say.

"If you're so opposed to marriage, why are you here?" he asked. "Did your father make you come?"

"No. I...." I stumbled, unsure what to say. He was watching me expectantly. I decided to tell him the truth. "I just wanted to see you one last time."

The song ended, but he didn't let me go. He had that same studious expression on his face, as if he was trying to figure me out. I held very still, wondering what exactly he was thinking. The moment seemed to last forever.

"Will you dance with me again?"

Nothing in the world could have made me happier. "Of course."

He smiled. He nodded at the musicians in the corner. A new song started. And we danced.

It was both nerve-racking and intoxicating being so close to him. Breasts—*my* breasts—were pressed tight between us. I found the feeling incredibly disconcerting, but everything else was perfect: the way he looked at me. The firmness of his hand on the small of my back. He stirred something in me—a dull, pulsing ache between my legs, so different from the feeling of arousal in my own body, and yet, unmistakably recognizable. It made my knees weak. My stomach was queasy, full of butterflies. Every piece of me strained toward him, longing for him in a way I'd never fully realized before. I felt feverish. My body—my *female* body—felt like it was burning up from the inside out. Surely he must sense it. Surely he must recognize the affect he was having on me.

He pulled me tighter against him, and I felt the stiffness of his member against me. It made me breathless. He tilted his head down to me, his lips a centimeter from my own.

"Would it be completely inappropriate if I kissed you?"

My heart soared. I put my arms around his neck and whispered back, "Appropriate is boring."

His mouth was warm and soft. His tongue teased against my lips, and I heard myself whimper. I opened up to him, letting him taste me, letting him explore me. He moaned, a low sound from deep in his throat that caused the heat between my legs to grow. The ache seemed to spread simultaneously down my thighs and up through my abdomen to the breasts that were jammed uncomfortably between us. The room ceased to exist. The music too. Whether the musicians stopped, whether they whispered, or whether they played on, I didn't know and didn't care. I hung onto him,

Cinder

wondering how something as simple as a kiss could feel so unbelievably good.

He broke the kiss, still holding me close. He was as breathless as I was.

"That was amazing," he gasped.

I could only cling to him and nod.

"Why do you seem so familiar?"

I shook my head, not wanting to let him think about it. Not wanting to think about how I should answer. I pulled his head down so I could kiss him again, but he stopped just before his lips met mine.

"What's your name?"

My name. What *was* my name? All that time I'd spent waiting my turn to dance with him, and it hadn't once occurred to me he might ask me such a simple question. I had no idea what to say. I couldn't think of anything except my *real* name. I couldn't give him that.

"Umm...." I said stupidly.

But I was saved from answering by a sound—a terrible, heartbreaking sound.

The sound of the bells in the clock tower striking midnight.

※

I fled. I ran from the ballroom, Xavier calling after me, first asking and then ordering me to wait.

I had no choice but to disobey.

Faces with wide eyes and gaping mouths turned as I sped past. I was vaguely aware of making such a ridiculous spectacle of myself, but it would be far worse if they saw me without the magic.

Somewhere on the stairs, the first of the spells gave way. One moment I was running in the ornate slippers, and the next I was tripping. The tall heels of the shoes threw my balance too far forward. My ankles wobbled. The movement of my hips became my own. "Plodding, clumsy men," the witch had said, and in the space of a few seconds, I'd become one again, albeit still hidden within the body of a woman. I fell halfway down the stairs, tearing my dress in the process.

How in the world did women manage?

Behind me, I could hear voices calling. Somebody was coming after me. I pulled the ridiculous sandals from my feet and ran. I ducked behind the row of waiting carriages. I was vaguely aware of coachmen and drivers, their eyes wide with shock, as I bolted past them.

"Guess that one's dance didn't end well," one of them laughed.

I ran all the way home, gasping for air against the constraints of the corset I wore, wishing I could tear the damn thing off, but the coachmen might do more than stare if the woman flying past them was bare-breasted.

Finally, I stumbled through our gate, but I stopped short on the walk. The light was on in the parlor. Aunt Cecile was waiting up, anxious for word from her daughters.

I couldn't let her see me—the specter of her dead sister, dress torn, feet bare and caked with mud. I could go in the back door, but even that seemed risky. What if she called to me to bring her tea or stoke the fire?

With a moan, I turned and headed for the only place I could think of. The only place that was mine: the clearing in the woods. The place I'd first met Xavier. The place where I'd met the witch.

The meadow was empty, of course. I fell to the ground in a graceless heap, glad to finally be able to sit. My side ached from running. My feet hurt. I'd lost a shoe somewhere along the way. I felt a bit bad about it. I hoped the witch wouldn't be mad.

It took a few minutes to catch my breath. The crickets had stopped their songs as I passed, but now they began again. Something skittered away unseen in the woods. It was quiet and peaceful. Moonlight shone through the trees, dappling the forest floor.

I wanted to undo the dress and loosen the corset, but the buttons were too high up my back for me to reach. After a minute of stretching and straining, I gave up. One more reason I was glad to not be a woman.

I leaned back against the fallen log Xavier had left his gift on. I'd traded that gift away for two spells, and a few short hours, but it had been worth it.

I thought about Xavier. I relived the dance. I remembered the feeling of him holding me close. The taste of him. The hardness of his erection against me. Heat kindled again in my groin, so familiar, and yet so strange. I remembered the soaring joy in my heart when he'd asked if he could kiss me.

I curled up on the soft leaves of the forest floor. And I thought again, as I drifted off to sleep, *It was worth it.*

<hr>

I slept fitfully at first, but at some point, the constriction around my chest ceased, the itchiness of the lace went away, and I fell into a comfortable slumber, at home in my own body.

I woke well after dawn. I was myself again, wearing my usual patched clothes. My feet were bare. My worn boots lay on the ground next to me.

On any other morning, I would have been up at dawn. I wondered if Aunt Cecile and my cousins were searching for me. Would they wonder where I'd gone? Would they care? I could only hope that after the late night, they'd all slept in.

I stopped by the well behind the house to clean myself off. My feet were scratched and dirty from my barefoot sprint home. I washed away the dried mud and pulled my boots on before heading inside.

I knew right away something was amiss. I could hear Jessalyn and Penelope in the living room, talking frantically over each other. Deidre turned to glare at me.

"Fine morning for you to be off missing," she said. "They're in a right uproar."

"Over what?"

She waved her hand at me dismissively as she turned back to her stove. "Something about the prince and the ball."

I had work to do. I had no reason to get involved. No reason at all.

Except she'd mentioned the prince. Whatever had my cousins in a 'right uproar,' it involved Xavier. Just the thought of him made my heart skip a beat. I knew I'd get nothing done until I discovered what was going on.

Penelope and Aunt Cecile rushed busily around the living room, dusting and straightening. It was something they usually left for Deidre and me to do. Jessalyn sat in her favorite chair, glaring at them as they worked.

"I don't know why you're bothering," she said. "We know he won't come here."

"We know no such thing," Aunt Cecile said. "They say he picked a bride, and he'll call on her today."

He'd picked a bride?

A sad knot of jealousy clenched inside my chest. Of course he'd picked a bride. That had been the entire purpose of the ball. Still, after the way he'd held me, and the kiss….

"Who is she?" I asked.

They all turned to me. They hadn't noticed me enter, and now they all stared at me as if I'd asked them who hung the moon.

"Nobody knows," Penelope said at last.

"She ran away," Jessalyn said.

"They say the prince was calling after her, but she didn't stop, and—"

"Yes," Jessalyn said, cutting her off. "And that's how we know it won't be one of us. We weren't fools enough to run away!"

My heart skipped a beat. Yes, I'd run away, because I'd had no other choice. Was there any possibility another girl had fled as well? Could he be searching for somebody other than me?

It seemed unlikely.

I didn't know whether to laugh or cry. "But he knows who she is?" I asked.

"They say he doesn't know her name, but he has a way to find her," Penelope said. "Everybody's talking about it."

A way to find her.

A way to find *me*?

I couldn't help myself. I burst out laughing.

Of course he was wrong. He couldn't find her, because she didn't exist. The woman he sought had disappeared in the night, nothing more than a spell. He could hunt, but he'd never catch his prey.

They were all staring at me in shock, and I realized I was still laughing. More than laughing. I was bordering on hysterical, holding my stomach, trying to use the laughter to keep my tears at bay.

He wanted to marry me.

"Cinder, *what* is so funny?" Aunt Cecile asked.

"Nothing," I said, gasping for air, trying to regain my composure. It was true. There was nothing funny about what was happening. "I'm sorry." Not that my apology helped. Aunt Cecile looked disgusted. My cousins, confused. "How will he find her?" I asked.

But before they could reply, I received my answer: the familiar baying of a dog. Everybody turned toward the front window. Penelope rushed over to peek through the curtains.

I didn't need to look. I knew what she would see.

Milton.

"Oh no," I moaned.

They all turned to me in surprise, but before they could ask what was wrong, there was a great, loud knock at the door.

Penelope's pale hand fluttered to her mouth, her eyes wide with excitement and fear. Aunt Cecile was practically bouncing in her shoes. Jessalyn rushed to the door and pulled it open.

A massive, hairy shape raced through the opening, barking and drooling. Milton flew at me, knocking me over backward on to the floor. His paws landed on my abdomen. His weight drove the air from my lungs as I hit the ground. His massive, quivering jaws loomed over my face.

"Milton, you hairy oaf!" a voice I recognized as Xavier's cried. "What's come over you?"

Milton moved off of my chest, and then the prince was looming over me, his face lit by his handsome smile.

"Eldon!" he cried happily. He took my hand and helped me to my feet. "I didn't expect to find you here."

Milton had knocked the wind out of me. I was too busy trying to breathe to answer. My stomach was cramped, my brain screaming for oxygen and apparently not comprehending that it needed only to inhale. I was vaguely aware of the room around me—my aunt and cousins, Deidre, who had come in from the kitchen, the two men who'd entered with Xavier. All of them wore shocked expressions, clearly wondering at the prince's familiar attitude toward a servant.

What wasn't vague at all was the gentle firmness of his hand on my back, so similar to the night before.

"Eldon," he said, "are you all right?"

I finally managed to take a short breath. And then a second. "I'm fine," I gasped, although I still couldn't quite stand up straight.

"I can't think why he bowled you over like that," he said.

Cinder

"He's always liked you, but still." He looked over at Milton, who sat by the fireplace, panting happily. His wagging tail thumped against the wooden floor. The steady *thump, thump, thump* seemed unusually loud in the otherwise quiet room. My aunt and cousins gaped at me, obviously baffled and wondering how Xavier knew my name.

I made myself stand tall, although my stomach still hurt. I turned to him and said, "Sire?" He lowered his eyebrows, glaring at me, and I knew he wanted to tell me not to call him that. I rushed on, before he could. "Perhaps you should tell us why you've honored us with a visit today?"

His eyes swept quickly over my aunt and my cousins, and Deidre, dismissing them each in turn. He glanced hopefully around the room, as if he may have missed somebody, then turned toward the stairs.

"I'm looking for somebody," he said. "Is there anybody else here? Upstairs, maybe?"

"No," I said. Of course I knew who he hoped to find, but it seemed he was waiting for me to say more, so I asked, "Who were you expecting?"

He smiled at me. "A girl." He reached into his coat and pulled something from his pocket. He held it up for me to see.

It was my lost shoe.

"I gave it to Milton," he said, "and Milton led me here."

He turned again to eye my cousins with unabashed curiosity, trying to determine if one of them was the girl he sought. He was confused, I could tell. I had resembled them both and yet, he seemed to not recognize them at all.

"Perhaps Milton was confused," I said.

Xavier shook his head in response. "Impossible. You know he's the best tracker in the kingdom."

Yes. So good he'd managed to track me through a magical sex-change.

Xavier held the shoe up for my cousins to see. In the

bright light of day, it looked sad. Wilted. The ornate lace straps seemed wretched. "Does this belong to either of you?"

The room was deathly silent, still as a tomb. Everybody's attention was on the shoe.

Penelope spoke first. "No, sire," she started to say. "It's not ours—"

Jessalyn cut her off. She stepped forward. Her twin sister was confused. Her mother, elated. I felt my heart sink in my chest.

She wouldn't be so low, would she? She wouldn't lie!

But I knew I was being a fool.

Of course she would.

She smiled at the prince and said, "Yes, Highness. It's mine."

Nobody moved. Xavier still held the shoe aloft as studied Jessalyn.

Something stirred in my chest—an angry rebellion. A hurt and jealous beast. How dare she?

"It's not your shoe," I said.

Xavier turned to me in surprise. Jessalyn's dark eyes fixed on me as well, demanding my silence.

"Of course it is."

Xavier glanced back and forth between us, obviously unsure how to proceed. "Perhaps," he said to Jessalyn, "if you could produce the other one?"

She blinked at him, smiling, and whether she really was confused by his question or whether it was an act, I didn't know. "The other one?" she asked.

"Yes," he said with seemingly infinite patience. "The other shoe. They usually come in pairs."

Her face flushed. Her eyes darted from side to side. Could he see the cold calculation in them?

"I lost them both, Sire," she said. "I was in such a hurry to get away, I couldn't run properly."

"Why exactly did you run?"

"Well…." She played nervously with the necklace she wore. She bit her lip. I'd never realized what a wonderful actress she was. "I was so nervous, Your Highness. Being in your presence…I'm afraid I was a bit overwhelmed."

Xavier's puzzlement grew. "Overwhelmed?" he said, as if contemplating the meaning of the word. I knew he was thinking about our dance. Thinking about the fact that, unlike so many of the other girls, I *hadn't* been overwhelmed by him. We'd talked of fishing. And magic.

And we'd kissed.

Jessalyn must have seen his hesitation. She must have sensed his uncertainty. She took another step toward him and said, "I'll prove it, Sire. Let me try on the shoe."

His face lit with a smile. "Wonderful idea!"

Jessalyn sat on the ottoman nearest the prince. She reached down and removed the boot she wore. She looked up at him expectantly.

Xavier held the slipper toward her.

Jessalyn crossed her legs, right over left, holding her bare foot toward him. She tugged her dress a bit, causing the lace-trimmed hem to slide alluringly upward, revealing her pale ankle.

Xavier's face flushed. It was clear she expected him to get on his knee in front of her and help her into the shoe. It was equally clear he had no intention of doing so. He held it out to Penelope.

"Assist her," he said. There was a note in his voice I'd never heard before—a tone of command. A tone he'd never used with me.

Jessalyn hid her disappointment well. Only years of living with her allowed me to see the quick blink of her eye that hinted at her dissatisfaction.

Penelope took the sandal from the prince and knelt at her sister's feet. She held it out. I could barely breathe. The air felt heavy with anticipation.

Jessalyn slid her foot neatly inside.

Something inside of me withered and died. Some dream I'd had. Some secret I'd buried so deep, even I hadn't quite known it was there. Jessalyn's pretty little foot in that stupid lace slipper was like a knife in my chest.

I wanted to throw myself at his feet. I wanted to tell him the truth.

I wanted desperately to be her.

Jessalyn beamed up at the prince. Xavier still seemed uncertain, but he smiled back. "I suppose this is the part where I ask for your hand in marriage."

She jumped up and threw her arms around his neck. He hesitated, but only for a second. He put his arms around her. He buried his nose in her thick, chestnut hair.

He looked happy.

I closed my eyes. I forced myself to breathe. I willed my heart to stop aching. So Jessalyn would have the man I loved as her own. What did it matter? It wasn't as if he could choose me anyway, even if he wanted to.

They were all talking at once. The room was so loud. Plans were already being made. Time was short. The prince had to take a wife by midnight, nine days hence. Jessalyn and Xavier would be leaving the very next morning, heading back to his home to plan the wedding. She'd see him every day. Every day for the rest of her life.

And me? I'd see him when they came to visit. *If* they came to visit.

"Eldon?"

It was Xavier's voice, and everybody else in the room stopped speaking. I could almost feel the weight of their stares as they turned to look at me.

I took a deep breath. I made myself open my eyes and face him. He was smiling. He put his hand on my shoulder. "You'll come, won't you?"

"Sire?"

He scowled at me. I knew he wanted to tell me to call him by his name, but after glancing quickly at Jessalyn, Penelope, and Aunt Cecile, he seemed to think better of it. They were all watching us, obviously listening to our conversation. He stepped closer to me, making me feel that what we shared was special. His hand on my shoulder felt warm and heavy. "It's a fortuitous day. Not only do I find my bride, I gain a brother, too." His voice was low, but it was so quiet in the room, everybody heard him. "It pleases me to have a reason to keep you near."

I ducked my head to hide my smile.

Maybe my heart wasn't so broken after all.

2

The king left for home that very day, as soon as he was assured of Xavier's impending marriage, and I spent the next twenty-four hours rushing around like a fool, trying to get Jessalyn and myself both ready to leave. Xavier offered to take Penelope and Aunt Cecile along too, but Jessalyn protested, saying she didn't want to trouble anyone. Her mother and sister were understandably furious. They were gracious enough not to say anything in front of the prince, but once he was gone, the accusations and arguments began. I was glad. They were all so busy snarking at each other, nobody thought to question me about my friendship with Xavier.

Jessalyn may have claimed she was leaving her family behind out of some misplaced sense of martyrdom, but I knew the truth: she didn't want anybody around who might embarrass her or remind others of her less-than-royal roots. She would certainly have left me behind as well, if she'd had the choice, but Xavier made it quite clear he wanted me along.

And so it was that I found myself on the way to the palace the very next morning, in the company of Xavier, Jessalyn, and a dozen guards and attendants.

And of course, Milton.

Jessalyn rode in a carriage with the prince. He'd started out on horseback like the rest of us, but she'd batted her eyes at him and made some simpering comment about getting to know one another better and he'd relented and joined her, tucked away inside the vehicle, out of sight, out of my reach.

I couldn't hear their conversation, but every so often, I'd hear Jessalyn laugh. I tried to tell myself the jealousy I felt each time was foolish. I told myself my growing hatred of her was unjustified. I wondered over and over again if I should tell the prince that Jessalyn was not who he thought.

We stopped at midday to eat. I helped two of the servants lay out a cold lunch of cheese, ham, biscuits, and fresh strawberries for Xavier and Jess while the other men tended to the horses and ate their own lunches of hard bread and dried meat. Milton eyed the picnic with an attentiveness that was downright alarming. Strings of drool hung from his heavy jowls. I was afraid if we turned away for even a second, he'd swallow the entire spread in one bite.

"Am I really supposed to sit on the ground?" Jessalyn asked. "I'd hate to ruin my gown."

Xavier regarded her with what seemed a mix of amusement and annoyance as she dispatched me to the carriage for cushions and a blanket in order to keep her dress clean.

I avoided his eyes as I helped her get settled across from him. I hated for him to see me as what I was—a mere servant to his bride-to-be. I was afraid I would look at him and see pity in his eyes.

"That's good enough," Jess said, making a shooing motion at me with her hands. "You can go."

I turned to leave, but I was stopped by a question from Xavier. "Why don't you join us, Eldon?" I turned to find him gesturing for me to sit next to him on the ground.

The question caught me by surprise. So did the expression on his face. There was no pity or disgust, as I'd expected. Only the same friendly regard I'd seen on his face every other time we'd been together. Whatever resentment

I'd felt for my cousin was wiped from my mind by the warmth of his smile and the sincerity of the invitation.

"Oh Xavier," Jessalyn said, and I wondered if I actually saw a wince of annoyance on his face when she said his name. "A servant lunching with the prince? That really wouldn't be appropriate."

He smiled over at her. "Appropriate is boring."

The statement made me laugh out loud, but Jessalyn only blinked at him in surprise. "On the contrary, I think it's important for us to maintain a sense of propriety when there are servants around."

The smile slowly faded from Xavier's face to be replaced by puzzlement. I knew he was thinking about our kiss, wondering if this woman he was talking to could possibly have forgotten having said those very words to him.

As much as I longed for time with the prince, I didn't want Jessalyn watching us and listening in. I wanted to keep my friendship with him to myself. I wanted to keep it out of the reach of her grasping fingers.

"Thank you for the invitation," I said, "but perhaps I should take care of Milton."

He was disappointed, I could tell, but Jessalyn said immediately, "Good idea, Cinder. Tie him up behind the carriage."

I did take Milton behind the carriage, but I didn't tie him up. Instead, I took off my boot, and the two of us played fetch until it was time to leave.

Xavier chose not to return to the carriage. Instead, he had his horse brought to him. "I'm going to ride ahead and make sure everything's ready at the inn," he said, motioning two of his guards to accompany him. Then he turned to me. "Eldon, will you join me?"

"I'd love to."

"Of course he'd love to, Xavier," Jessalyn said, "but it will have to be another day."

This time, I was sure I saw a flash of annoyance in Xavier's eyes, although it was gone by the time he turned to her. "And why is that?"

She seemed to sense his impatience. She immediately turned on the 'poor me' routine, ducking her head and glancing up at him through her long lashes. She gestured to the rest of the guard. "I don't know any of these men," she said. "You wouldn't leave me in the company of strangers, would you?"

"Do you suspect any of them would be fool enough to harm you?"

"Of course not," she said. "It's just that I'd feel so much more comfortable if Cinder were here with me."

I clenched my hands tight on the reins of my horse. I ducked my head so they couldn't see my expression. I hated to be caught between them, not because I didn't know which direction I preferred, but because I knew the more Xavier pushed, the more miserable Jess would endeavor to make me.

The prince sighed. "Fine," he relented. "I'll see you in a few hours."

He turned without another word and left us, Milton running ahead with a triumphant howl, the two guards following behind.

I was left alone with Jess and ten men I did not know.

With the prince gone, Jessalyn dropped her act in an instant. She turned to me with fury in her eyes. "Get in the carriage, Cinder," she said. "It's time you and I had a talk."

The carriage was awful. Jessalyn had the curtains closed on the one small window, making it dark and stuffy inside. I sat across from her. The space was way too small. I could feel the anger and resentment coming off of her, filling the carriage, making it hard to breathe. I wished I could scoot back and put more distance between us. I thought of how uncomfortable the ride must have been for Xavier, who was several inches taller than me. No wonder he'd decided to ride his horse for the second half of the day.

Jessalyn waited until we were well underway before she spoke. I knew she hoped the sound of the wheels and the road and the horses would prevent the guardsmen from overhearing.

"How do you know the prince?" she asked, her voice pitched low.

"I met him in the forest."

Disbelief flashed in her eyes. "Doing what?"

I didn't know if she meant him or me, so I answered both possibilities. "I was going to the river to fish, and he was playing fetch with Milton."

"And then what? He just decided to talk to you?"

"He asked if he could go fishing with me."

"A *prince* asked a *servant* if he could go fishing?"

"Yes."

"Why? What lies did you tell him?"

"I only told him the truth."

She slapped me. In all the years I'd been part of my aunt's household, she'd never struck me, and it took me completely by surprise.

"Don't lie to me!"

I put my hand to my cheek, as if I could hold the sting of her wrath there. I savored her anger and her jealousy. I had no desire to appease her. "You know all about lying, don't you?"

She went very still. The only movement was the flaring of her nostrils.

"Shall we talk about the shoe?" I asked. "We both know it doesn't belong to you."

"Are you threatening me?"

Was I? Even I wasn't sure. But she didn't give me a chance to answer.

"Think about this, *Eldon*." She'd never called me that before, and I knew she only did it now to remind me of the prince's familiarity with me. "If you tell him, and he believes you, what happens then? Have you thought about that?"

"He'll pick a new bride."

"Yes. And I'll be sent home. And where do you think you'll be?" She smiled at me—a cruel, malicious smile that made my blood run cold—and she gave me the answer. "You'll still be working for me. And I promise you, Cinder, I will spend the rest of my life making yours a living hell."

It was true. It made me sick to my stomach to admit it, but she was right. Unless….

"He might not send me away."

She laughed, and if I'd thought her smile was cruel, her laughter was worse. "When he learns you've allowed this to go on as long as it has, do you think you'll still have his favor?"

It was a good question. Would I? Or would he blame me for not telling him sooner?

"Do you honestly think you can fool him forever?" I asked.

"I don't need to fool him forever. We'll be married in eight days. After that, it'll be too late." She leaned back in her seat. She crossed her arms. She looked smug. She thought she'd won.

Of course, she had. I hated it, but she had a point. I hung my head in defeat.

She knocked on the side of the carriage, and it slowed to a stop.

"Get out of my carriage, *Cinder*," she said. "And if you know what's good for you, you'll keep your secrets to yourself."

The rest of the afternoon was miserable. It was blistering hot. We were plagued by flies. By the time we reached the inn, I was sweaty, stinky, and sunburned. Even the scene with Jessalyn paled when I thought about the bliss of a home-cooked meal and a night in a soft bed.

If it was hot outside, I could only imagine how stifling it had been inside the carriage. I was happy to see that even Jessalyn couldn't emerge unscathed. Her dress was damp and wrinkled. She was sullen and cranky. And she smelled no better than I.

Xavier greeted us at the door. He'd had dinner laid out in a private room near the back.

"I brought champagne," he said, pouring not two, but three glasses. "It's perfectly chilled." He held a glass out to her. "It will refresh you."

"Thank you, my Prince," Jessalyn said as she reached for the glass.

Xavier teasingly pulled it out of her reach. "Do you intend to curtsy like a proper lady?" he asked.

Jessalyn actually blushed up to her sweaty hairline. "My apologies, Highness," she said, as she bent her knee. "Please forgive my oversight."

The surprise on Xavier's face might have made me laugh any other time, but this time, it only served to remind me that keeping Jessalyn's secret was in my own best interest.

"I think the prince was joking, my lady," I said.

"Of course," Xavier said, taking her hand and bringing her to her feet. "But I shouldn't have. After such a long day, it was in terrible taste."

She smiled sweetly at him as she took the champagne. "Thank you." He watched her expectantly as she took a small sip. She seemed to realize he was anticipating some kind of reaction from her, but she obviously didn't know what. She smiled uncertainly at him. "It's interesting," she said. "I've never tasted anything like it."

He was clearly disappointed, but he didn't say anything. He took the second glass from the table and offered it to me. "Have some, Eldon," he said. "I'm sure you could use a drink, as well."

I took a sip, and I discovered why he'd watched Jessalyn's reaction so attentively. It was the same champagne he'd served to me at the ball. I was immediately transported back to that night by the bright, bubbly sensation of sunlight on my tongue, and I did as I'd done then—I tilted my head back and drank it all at once.

"It's delicious!" I said as I handed him my empty glass.

He laughed. "I'm glad somebody appreciates it." I didn't miss the scowl this elicited from my cousin, but the prince didn't seem to notice. "Would you like more?" he asked me.

"No," Jessalyn said, answering for me. "Cinder needs to help me freshen up for dinner."

I did as instructed. After that, I rushed around while she dined with the prince. I helped the guardsmen with the luggage, doing my best to swallow a few bites of dinner between trips up and down the stairs. I had to constantly rush to the dining room to attend to Jessalyn, who couldn't seem to let a moment pass without reminding the prince and me both of my true station.

Through it all, I saw the prince's puzzlement grow. I saw the way he scrutinized her, and the way he grew distant as she prattled on, alternately flattering him and assuring him what a wonderful wife she'd be.

Finally, the meal ended, and Jessalyn excused herself for the night. Xavier stood and kissed her hand. Then, as she made her way to the door, he turned to me. "Sit with me, Eldon," he said. "Help me finish this champagne."

His invitation made me grin. "I'd love to."

But of course, Jessalyn couldn't bear to leave me with

him. "I'm afraid I need Cinder with me."

"I thought you were going to bed," Xavier said, raising his eyebrows at her. "Certainly you don't require Eldon's assistance there?"

The suggestion caused Jess and me both to blush. "Of course not," Jessalyn said. "But I want to take a bath first. I need Cinder to haul up the water."

"I'm sure someone from the inn can assist you."

She put her shoulders back and flipped her hair back in defiance. "I won't allow strangers into my room."

Xavier's expression turned skeptical. He cocked his head back a bit. I knew he was debating whether to give in or not.

"Sire?" By turning further toward him, putting my back to Jessalyn, I was able to grant us the illusion of privacy. I pitched my voice low, hoping she wouldn't be able to hear. "I'll find you later."

The smile that bloomed on his face was broad and beautiful. "I'd like that," he said, matching my hushed tone. What I saw in his eyes as he said it made the color rise on my cheeks. It made my heart leap inside my chest. It wasn't romantic, or suggestive. It was simply the sincerity of his desire to see me, and to spend time with me. It made me ache in a way that was both exhilarating and heartbreaking.

He was the wind, and I would take whatever little bit of him I could reach.

"Who do you think you are?" Jessalyn raged at me, once we were alone in her room. "Drinking champagne with him! Sitting at the table as if you were equals!"

"He invited me."

"It's pathetic!" she practically spat the word at me. "Here on the road, where there are only guards around, he may treat you like a friend, but once we're at the palace, he'll

Cinder

forget you. And then I'll send you home."

Her words stung, because there was a chance she was right. At the palace, he probably had other friends—men who really were his equal in every way. But there was no point in worrying about it, and there was even less point in arguing.

I ignored everything she said after that. I kept my head down and I did my job. She railed on, throwing barbs at me, telling me I was a fool, telling me I was nothing. I didn't say a word, and eventually she gave up on goading me.

When the bath was done and I'd hauled away the tub, I bid her good night and turned to leave.

"I didn't say you could go. I won't have you running off to tell the prince lies about me."

My grip on the doorknob tightened. My knuckles were white. "I know where I stand," I said through clenched teeth. "You made things quite clear today in the carriage."

"I still don't trust you."

"There doesn't seem to be much I can do about that."

"I could order you to stay."

My patience was at an end. Yes, I worked for her, but she didn't own me. I turned to face her. "I'm leaving," I said. "Go ahead and yell. Go ahead and scream. Let the whole damn inn hear you rage. Do you really think that will help? Do you think the prince will think better of you when you're done?"

She opened her mouth to speak, but no sound came out. It seemed I'd finally struck her speechless. I did my best not to gloat as I left her.

I stood outside Xavier's door for a long time, willing my heart to stop racing. Trying to work up enough courage to knock.

The door opened before I had a chance.

"Eldon, what are you doing standing out here in the hallway? Come in, for heaven's sake!" He took my hand and pulled me inside, closing the door behind me. "I'm afraid I finished the champagne without you. Rude, I know, but it seemed the best way to kill the time."

"It's fine," I said. "I'm not really used to drinking anyway."

"Did she finally let you go?"

Not exactly, but it didn't seem worthwhile to go into it. "I think she's gone to bed."

He shook his head, turning away from me as if he couldn't bear to face me. "Do you think I'm crazy?" he asked.

"Why would I think that?"

"For marrying her?"

"Not crazy. Just…." I wasn't really sure how to finish my sentence. Misled? Taken by his faithful dog to the right house, but the wrong woman?

"Yes?" he prodded. "Go on. Tell me what you think."

What exactly could I say? "I think whatever happened at the ball must have made quite an impression."

"Yes. It was extraordinary." The fondness of the memory made his voice soft. "I wish I could tell you about that night and have you understand."

Of course I already knew all about that night, but the idea of hearing it from his perspective intrigued me. "Why wouldn't I?"

"It's only that it seems so crazy. It was…." He shook his head. "It was like magic."

I found myself smiling. "You don't believe in magic."

He laughed grudgingly. "I know." He pushed his hair back from his forehead and sighed. "But there was something about her. Something so *familiar*. Like I already knew her."

His words seemed to warm me from the inside. It *had* been magical.

"I kissed her." He glanced at me sideways, as if he expected me to disapprove.

"And?"

"It was like nothing else I've ever experienced. It was like coming home. It was…." He shook his head. "I can't describe it."

But I didn't need him to describe it. I remembered the taste of him, the feel of his lips against on mine, the tightness of his arms around me, the soft moan he'd made as we'd kissed. "It was amazing."

"Excuse me?"

His words shook me out of my reverie. He was staring at me in surprised amusement. "Oh." I'd been so lost in my memory of that night. I hadn't meant to speak at all. "I'm sorry. I didn't mean to be presumptuous."

He shook his head. "Don't apologize, Eldon. You're right. Everything about that night was amazing." He reached into his satchel. He pulled out the shoe and held it for me to see. It looked a bit worse for the wear. "I was ecstatic when I found this. Between it and Milton, I had a way to find her."

At the sound of his name, Milton rose from his place by the fire. He padded over to his master, his tail wagging.

Xavier held the shoe down to him. "Milton: find."

Milton took the shoe in his mouth. He plodded over to me and dropped the shoe at my feet.

Xavier shook his head with obvious confusion. "Maybe he's not such a good tracker after all."

"Well," I said shakily, "he led you to our house."

"To your marriageable cousin." His tone was lighthearted, and yet I knew it pained him.

"You don't want to marry her?"

"I want to marry the girl I danced with." He shook his head again. "The girl I kissed."

"You don't believe Jessalyn is that girl?"

He moaned in frustration. "I don't know. I suppose she must be. Milton led me to her. She's the right height. Her hair is as I remember. Her face…. Well, the lighting in the ballroom was poor, and I'd already danced with more than a dozen girls, and I'll admit I'd had a glass or two of champagne. It *must* be her. And yet...."

"And yet?" I prodded, when I realized he didn't intend to go on.

"I thought that when I saw her, it would be as magical as it was at the ball. That I'd recognize her immediately, like being struck by lightning."

"But it wasn't."

"Not even close."

He sat down on the one chair in the room, his elbows on his knees and his head in his hands. I'd never seen him so beaten.

I had to tell him the truth. Whatever Jessalyn had said to me in the carriage was irrelevant. I couldn't lie to him any longer. I was terrified—my heart hammered painfully inside my chest, and my palms began to sweat—but I knew it was the right thing to do.

"Sire?" My voice shook. "What if I told you that you're right? That Jessalyn isn't the right girl."

He looked up at me, his eyes bright with hope. "You know who she is?"

I do. That's what I tried to say, but the words wouldn't come out. He was watching me expectantly, and I forced myself to nod.

"Go on."

"This will sound crazy, but—"

"For heaven's sake, Eldon, tell me!"

I took a deep breath and said, "It was me. I traded the fish you left me to the witch, and she turned me into a girl for one night so I'd have a chance to say goodbye."

My words seemed to echo in the silence. He was surprised at first, but it quickly gave way to confusion, and then his eyes hardened in a way I'd never seen before. "I suppose you think that's funny," he said as he stood up and

Cinder

turned away from me. "It's easy for you to joke. It's not your life."

He didn't believe me. Of course he didn't. Why would he? It was utterly absurd.

I opened my mouth to speak. I could convince him. I could recount that evening, and the dance, and the conversation we'd had. That's all it would take.

But then I thought forward to what would come once he *did* believe me.

He could not marry me. The girl he longed for would still be gone. Jessalyn was right about one thing: if he chose not to marry her, we'd likely both be sent away, and he'd be forever out of my reach. I'd never see him again. The thought caused my breath to catch in my throat.

I couldn't bear to leave him now.

If he married Jess, I'd at least be with him. I'd still have his friendship. My temporary resolve to tell him the truth died in my chest. Being with him in any capacity was more important to me.

"I'm sorry, Sire," I said, deliberately using a title instead of his name. "I shouldn't have made light of the situation. I was only trying to make you laugh."

He took a deep breath and let it out in a rush. His shoulders fell, and when he turned to face at me, he was almost smiling. "Don't call me 'Sire.'"

"Yes, Sire."

He laughed sheepishly. "You won't tell her what I've said, will you?"

He could have ordered me not to speak of it. Instead, he was asking for my silence. Asking me to keep his secret, as if we were equals. Asking as my friend. "I would never betray you." I wondered if he could hear my love for him in those few words.

He crossed the room to put his hand on my shoulder. He looked down into my eyes. "You're a good friend,

Eldon," he said. "It will be worth marrying your cousin to keep you near."

I ducked my head so he would so he wouldn't see how his words affected me. I didn't know if the feeling welling up inside my chest was joy or anguish. I didn't know if I should laugh or cry. My eyes ached with unshed tears, and I shut them tight in effort to keep them at bay.

It would be worth seeing her married to him, if it allowed me moments like this.

We arrived at the palace the next day. Jessalyn and I were each assigned rooms. I was surprised to find that mine wasn't in the servant quarters as I'd expected, but in the main wing. It was vast and sumptuous. The curtains were velvet and the sheets were made of silk. It was luxurious to the extreme. Jessalyn was outraged when she found out, mostly because I was closer to Xavier than she was. I knew it annoyed it her to no end. The entirety of my worldly possessions only filled one drawer of the massive armoire. I felt completely out of place.

My assumption that the prince had peers at the palace was quickly dispelled. True, there was a large group of young men and women who attempted to follow him and dote on him and catch his attention, but he managed to avoid them more often than not.

"They're not my friends," he told me, when I referred to them as such. "They'd each throw me to the wolves in a minute, if I wasn't my father's son."

For his part, Xavier seemed to have resigned himself to marriage. He spent most of his time with Jessalyn, planning the wedding.

Jessalyn's resolve to keep me away from the prince was stronger than ever. She kept me busy from dawn until dusk.

Cinder

She sent me on errands that kept me running from one end of the palace to the other. She sent me to town, sometimes three times in a day. She sent servants to find me and issue orders. Several times the orders were to undo what I'd just spent the whole morning doing. There was no rhyme or reason to her instructions, save one: keep me from Xavier. And at that, she succeeded, for a few days at least.

Late on the fourth day, I returned from town with a new shawl Jessalyn had commissioned just as she and Xavier were finishing dinner.

"It's absolutely the wrong size," she said when I showed it to her. "And I specifically told her to use the green, not the blue. Take it back at once."

I barely even heard her. I couldn't take my eyes off the prince.

He was smiling at me, that bright infectious smile that made me feel like I could fly.

"It's good to finally see you, Eldon. How have you been?"

I've missed your face and your voice and our afternoons fishing. I miss hearing you laugh. I'd given anything to have you to myself, if only for an hour. But I couldn't say any of that. Instead, I took a deep breath and said, "I'm good, Sire. Thank you for asking. It's wonderful to see you."

He lowered his eyebrow at me in a playful scowl. "Don't call me 'Sire.'"

"Yes, Sire."

The corner of his mouth twitched in amusement. "You look well."

"Thank you, Sire. Xavier. So do you." It was a lie, though. He *didn't* look well at all. The smile he gave me appeared to be genuine, but the one he turned on Jessalyn was fake. I could see the strain of the impending marriage in the tightness of his shoulders and the dark circles under his eyes.

He was obviously miserable.

"Cinder," Jessalyn said, shoving the shawl back into my hands, "this is unacceptable. Take it back now. Tell her I won't put up with shoddy work. If she can't do it right, I'll take my business someplace else."

Did she see the way the prince frowned at her? Did she see the way his expression darkened with disapproval?

"Surely it can wait until morning," he said.

She shook her head. "I intended to wear this to the engagement party the day after tomorrow," she said. "It's her own fault for getting it wrong."

And so I took myself back to town to inform the poor seamstress that my cousin had changed her mind about both the size and color, but was too arrogant to admit it.

The next day, I had a plan. I scheduled my tasks well. I timed everything perfectly. I picked up the new shawl early, but waited until the prince's dinner with Jessalyn was ending to present it. I let myself quietly through the dining room door. They were talking, and neither of them seemed to notice me.

"I can't believe they served us fish," Jessalyn complained.

Xavier blinked at her, clearly trying to maintain an expression of polite interest. "I requested it," he said. "I was under the impression you liked it."

"Certainly not. Your father's right. It's peasant food."

"But I thought you liked fishing?" he said. "At the ball, you said—"

"I have your new shawl," I said, stepping forward and cutting off the disastrous conversation. Jessalyn looked up at me with obvious annoyance. And Xavier?

He smiled at me again, as he had the day before. It seemed to warm me, all the way to my toes.

"Two days in a row, Eldon," he said. "We might make a habit out of this."

Cinder

Jessalyn snatched the shawl from my hands and inspected it. "I suppose it will do," she said.

"I think it's lovely," Xavier said to her. "The color suits you."

She batted her eyes at him, simpering. I envisioned ripping her hair out of her pretty head. "Thank you, Xavier."

He winced when she said his name, although he hid it by wiping his face with his napkin. "Well," he said, putting the linen down and pushing his chair back. "I think I'll bid you good night." He stood. She held her hand out to him, and he took it and dutifully kissed the back of it.

Then he turned to me.

"Eldon, will you join me for a drink?"

I tried to keep my expression neutral, lest Jessalyn see my happiness and try to thwart me. But this was what I'd hoped for. This was the reason I'd planned my day so carefully, waiting until after dinner to find him. I'd hoped he'd have a few moments to spend with me. "I'd love to—" I started to say. But of course Jessalyn cut me off.

"He can't," she said. "I need him to prepare my bath."

She was still seated at the table, and when Xavier turned to face her, I could see how little patience he had left for her.

"I'm sure somebody else can assist you."

"You know how I feel about letting strangers into my room."

"This is your home now," he said. "They're not strangers. They're servants, and they're paid to serve."

"I don't know who to ask—"

"Find. Somebody. Else."

"Yes, but Cinder is *my* servant."

His jaw clenched. He took a deep breath and said with the still calmness of barely controlled rage, "He's more than your servant. He's your cousin. And he's *my* friend."

"Surely you have other friends—"

She might have slapped him, his reaction was so sudden

and so strong. He pulled himself up to his full height and looked down at her with disdain. "I am your future husband," he said, his voice like ice. "More than that, I am your prince. I desire an hour or two with your *servant*. Is that *really* too much to ask? It costs you nothing. Are you truly unable to grant me such a simple request?"

She stared up at him with wide eyes. She had gambled, and she had lost, and now she had pushed him too far. I could see her sorting through her options, trying to decide how to appease him. But whatever she was to do, he had no interest in hearing it.

"With me, Eldon," he said.

It wasn't a request. It was an order. Possibly the first he'd ever given me. I had no choice but to follow. He was a river, and I was a leaf caught in his current. I let him carry me out the door. Down the hall.

Away from Jessalyn.

His anger faded quickly once we were in the hall. He sighed heavily. "I'm sorry you had to see that," he said. "I'm sorry you have to be involved."

"It's not your fault."

"It feels like it is. This whole damn mess is because of me."

"I could say the same thing about myself," I said. *Or Jessalyn.*

"I've missed you."

It wasn't sentimental. It wasn't shy. It was said with the same casual sincerity he might use to say, "The sky is blue," or "The sun is bright." There was no embarrassment and no apology. Only a simple statement of fact.

"I've missed you, too," I said. And I knew I'd failed to sound as casual as he.

We reached his room and he led me inside. Milton jumped off the bed with a howl and launched himself at me. His massive forepaws landed on my chest, and I fell back

Cinder

against the door as he tried to lick my face.

"Milton, off!" Xavier scolded.

Milton sighed and dropped dutifully to all four paws. I scratched his ears as a reward.

"I guess he missed you, too," Xavier said as he removed his dinner jacket and tossed it onto his bed. He gestured at a sumptuous armchair near the door. "Have a seat. Relax."

I followed the first order, and attempted to follow the second. The chair was deep and soft, and I could almost have slept in it. Milton turned and disappeared through a door into what must have been Xavier's closet.

"I should have brought some champagne," Xavier said. "Or some wine."

"It's fine. I don't usually drink."

"You keep saying that. I intend to change it." He ran his hands through his hair and scowled. "Frankly, I'd love to get drunk enough to forget this impending marriage, if only for a night."

I wasn't sure there was enough alcohol in the world for that, but I didn't answer. He didn't seem to be in the mood for jokes.

Milton emerged from the closet. He had something in his mouth. He looked quite determined, even for a dog. He plodded straight over to me and dropped his prize in my lap.

It was the shoe.

"Milton," Xavier scolded with obvious exasperation. "What is it with you and that slipper?"

Milton cocked his head at his master, as if to say, "What do you mean?"

"Oh, that damn thing!" Xavier swore, turning away to put his head in his hands. "If I hadn't found it, I wouldn't be in this mess."

"You'd still be getting married."

He sighed and scrubbed his hands over his face. "I suppose you're right, but at least it would have been a girl of my choosing. But now...."

"You still doubt she's the right girl."

He reached down and took the shoe from me, staring at it as if it held the answer. "I don't just 'doubt,' Eldon. I *know*. Everything about her is wrong: the way she laughs and the way she tries to flatter me and the way she bats her eyelashes and the things she says, and the way she—" He stopped short, and I knew there was something else.

"Yes?" I prompted. "And what?"

He turned to look at me. His cheeks were red. "The way she tastes," he said, his voice quiet. "I know that sounds crude, but I kissed her. I wanted to see if it felt like it did that night."

"But it didn't?"

"No. Not even close."

I didn't know what to say. All the questions that had plagued me since the day Jessalyn had slipped her foot into the shoe were running circles in my mind. Should I try once again to tell him? Would he believe me? What good could it possibly do anyway?

"Damn it all," he swore in frustration, throwing himself backward onto his bed. He glared again at the slipper in his hand. "How could this have happened, Eldon? How could it have gone so wrong?" He sat up and pointed the shoe at me. "She ran, as if the devil himself were after her. I chased her out the door, and I found this. I gave it to Milton." He looked down at Milton, who glared at him with barely disguised disgust. "He's supposed to be the finest tracking dog in the kingdom. When I gave it to him, he gave all the signs of having the trail, but...." He stopped, staring down forlornly at the shoe. "He led me straight to your house, Eldon. Straight to Jessalyn."

No, not to Jessalyn. To me. But how could I tell him that?

"Milton, come."

Milton went obediently to his master.

Xavier held the shoe out to Milton. "Milton: find."

Milton huffed. He took the slipper in his heavy, wet jowls. He padded across the room. He dropped the sodden thing in my lap, then turned his mournful doggy gaze to the prince.

"Every time!" Xavier said, laughing bitterly. "Every time, he leads me straight to you! It makes no sense! It's as if...." He stopped, his expression going from confused to contemplative. "As if...."

He stared at me, lost in thought.

"Straight to you," he said again.

My heart raced. My palms were suddenly damp. He stood up, staring at me, his eyes full of wonder and surprise. My mouth went dry.

"Your eyes," he said, his voice barely a whisper.

I ducked my head, suddenly unable to stand the weight of his gaze upon me. I didn't know if I wanted him to discover the truth or not. I hated lying to him, but if he knew Jessalyn was the wrong person, he'd refuse to marry her. He'd choose another bride, and I'd lose him.

"Look at me," he said, giving me an order for the second time that night. It took every ounce of my will to obey. His intensity was disconcerting. I couldn't think. I could barely breathe. He stepped up to my seat and held his hand down to me. "Dance with me."

I had to force myself to speak. "Sire?" My voice didn't sound right at all. It was entirely too rough, and too shaky.

"You heard me," he said. "Dance with me."

I rose, although my knees shook. He took my right hand in his left. He put his arm around my waist. It made my heart race, being so close to him again. "Are you ready?" he asked.

"No."

"Yes, you are," he said. "Now."

He started to dance. It should have been easy. He was

leading. I had only to follow. But I failed. The first step I managed to fake. The second, I went the wrong way, but corrected quickly. The third, I went forward when I should have gone back, and we ran into each other.

"Again," he said, but I'd lost any semblance of grace. As soon as he started to move again, I stumbled and nearly fell, stepping on his foot in the process.

"Eldon, what are you doing?"

"I don't know how to dance."

Only a few words, yet the change they caused him was profound. He was shocked, and hurt. "But...." He let me go, backing up a step, obviously confused. "That can't be."

I didn't know what to say, and I watched as he went from confused to defeated, his eyes going dark, his shoulders slumping. "Sire?"

"Stop calling me that!"

"Xavier—" But before I could say more, he waved my words away.

"I'm sorry," he said, turning away from me. "I was being a fool. I don't know what I was thinking."

But I *did* know what he'd been thinking, and the infuriating thing was, he'd been right. I'd tried to tell him once, but he hadn't believed me. I still didn't know what I had to gain by convincing him of the truth, but I hated to see him so lost. I wanted to touch him. I longed to dance with him again, even if it meant tripping over my own feet. I wanted him to look at me with that bright, astounded expression.

"It was the magic," I said.

It was barely a whisper. It was a miracle he heard me, but he did.

He turned to me, his eyes wide. "That's what she said, when I complimented her dancing."

"I know."

He didn't answer, but I could tell he was considering it

Cinder

again, replaying the night in his mind, trying to decide if it was possible. He stepped closer. He put his finger under my chin and tilted my head back, forcing me to meet his eyes. He used his other hand on the small of my back to pull me closer. "Could it be?" he asked.

Yes! I wanted to cry. *Yes, it could be, and it is!* But before I could answer, he kissed me.

His lips were soft. His touch was light. It was just as it had been on the dance floor—my legs shaking and unsteady, the gentleness of his hand on my back. The surety that I was only still standing because he held me up. I put my arms around his neck and opened myself up to him. His tongue touched my lips, testing—*tasting*—and I whimpered. He moaned in response, putting both of his arms around me, pulling me tight against him, kissing me deeper.

This was how it should be—chest to chest, not with the strange sensation of breasts pressed between us, but as two men, groin to groin, the proof his arousal hard against me. When he pulled back to look at me, his eyes were full of wonder.

"It *is* you!"

"I tried to tell you. I only wanted to see you again. I missed you that day in the woods, and I just wanted to say goodbye." The words spilled out of me, tumbling over each other in their haste to finally be free. "The witch did the spell, but I never meant for any of this to happen. I never expected you to choose me. I just wanted one dance. I didn't want you to leave without seeing you one last time. And so I went to the ball, and we were dancing, and it was all so perfect, but then the spell wore off, and I had to leave in such a hurry, and I lost the shoe. And then you showed up the next day with Milton, and I had no idea what to do."

"Why didn't you tell me?"

"I tried to, that night at the inn, but you didn't believe me. And I was so worried you'd send me away. I can't bear for you to send me away, Xavier. Please let me stay—"

He kissed me, cutting off my breathless plea. There was no hesitation. Only urgency. His kiss was a demand. An order. His fingers fumbled at the buttons on my shirt, and then my belt. He pushed me back on the bed. Part of me worried having this much of him now would only make it hurt more when I lost him, but I had no power to resist him. I was overwhelmed, as I so often was in his presence, the sheer force of his will propelling me forward, carrying me where he wanted me to be. I could only cling to him and trust he'd see me safely to the other side. I was lost in him—the weight of him on top of me, the way he tasted, the sounds he made, the softness of his lips, and insistence of his hands.

Lord, his *hands*.

They seemed to be everywhere, touching and teasing, and just when I thought the pleasure must surely peak and burn out, he'd shift his focus, touch me someplace new, ignite some yet unknown spark of desire within me, fanning it into a flame, stoking it into a wildfire that burned me up and consumed me.

When it was over, we lay spent and breathless, the sticky wetness of our pleasure cooling between us. His arms were tight around me, his face buried in my neck. I was glad he couldn't see the dampness on my cheeks.

"Eldon," he whispered, "what in the world are we going to do?"

3

I slept there with him, his arms tight around me as if he thought I might try to escape. Not that I had any intention of doing so. It was a peacefulness I had never known, curled up against his strong body, the brush of his breath on the back of my neck. Knowing he cared for me, on some level at least.

He woke me once in the night, rousing me from the depths of slumber, raising me again to the heights of pleasure. His mouth was warm and sweet and his hands were gentle yet insistent. He was firm in his desire. I could not have told him no. And yet what he seemed to want most was to please me.

I wished morning would never come. There was no price I wouldn't have paid for a magic that would have let my night with him last forever. But it was not to be.

I woke to the bells of the tower. It was six o'clock. The glow of morning sunlight through the curtains made the room feel soft and somehow secretive. Xavier was already up, sitting in the chair I'd occupied the night before, watching me. He didn't say a word.

For the first time, I felt awkward with him. He had a robe on, but I was still naked. I was painfully aware of the tan lines on my skin—most of my body was pale, but my arms, face and the back of my neck were bronze, betraying the hours I'd spent working in the sun. I hated the callouses on my hands. I was ashamed of my often-patched clothes as

I hurriedly pulled them on. His silence seemed ominous.

I finally turned to face him. A billion questions and hopes and worries stormed through my mind. Did he regret it? Did he want to see me again? Was it a one-time thing? I didn't even know how to leave. Was I to be kissed, as his lover? Bid goodbye, as a friend? Or excused, like a servant? Or worse, like a whore?

I could tell nothing by his eyes.

"Sire?" I wished my voice didn't shake. I wished I still felt as sure with him as I had before he'd taken me to his bed.

He smiled at me, but only a barely. It was a thin, sad smile. "Don't call me that."

"Xavier—"

He stood suddenly, cutting me off. "I'll break off the engagement today."

My heart stopped beating. I could barely make myself breathe, let alone speak. His words felt like the end of everything I'd hoped for. "Why?"

"Why?" His voice was hard and bitter, and I instinctively took a step back. "Why do you think?"

"You have to take a wife—"

"She's not the girl I want!" He stepped closer to me. His anger gave way to something gentle. He brushed his fingers over my cheek. "She's not the one I love."

If my heart had stopped beating before, it kicked into high speed now. "You love me?"

He smiled at me. He put his arms around me and pulled me close. "Eldon, you have no idea how many times I wanted to touch you, or to kiss you, but I was afraid you'd be horrified. If I'd only known...." He kissed my neck. His hand caressed my back. "Now that I do, we can be together. The way we should be."

A ridiculous, giddy grin threatened my composure. But I knew he wasn't seeing the whole picture.

"And what about your crown?"

He froze, his lips still against the pounding pulse in my neck, and I knew I was right. He hadn't thought it through. "Who cares?" he said at last. "I don't need it."

"So you'll give up your title and your inheritance? Leave the palace? Renounce your claim to your family's money and all the luxuries that go with it?"

I was challenging him now, and he took a step back, standing up straight, putting his shoulders back, the way he always did when somebody questioned his authority. "Yes. Why not?"

"Have you thought about what that would be like?"

"I don't need to. All that matters is that we'd be together."

The fact that he'd consider giving up his title for me was astounding. It made my heart swell inside my chest. It made me feel like I could fly.

But I knew he'd regret it in the end.

"What would we do? Live in my aunt's house, both of us as servants? I'm not even paid a salary."

His certainty began to fade as he considered my words. "Then we'll leave."

"And go where? What would you have us do? It's true, I could find a spot in another house. You could find work as a clerk maybe, or a tutor. We might make enough between us to get a room in town, at a boarding house. Is that what you want? To live like a peasant?" My words hurt him. I could see it. But he had to consider the consequences of his rash decisions. "No more horses. No more afternoons spent playing fetch with Milton. No more custom riding boots or exquisite meals. No more champagne that tastes like sunlight." That statement seemed to confuse him, but I rushed on. "No money. No title. Nothing. I'm glad you like fish, Xavier, because we'd be eating it nearly every day. Is that how you want to live? Do I mean so much to you as that?"

He wilted—there was no other way to put it. He slumped down into his chair with his head in his hands.

"What do you suggest?"

"Marry her," I said. "Marry anyone. Take the wife your father's law demands." He looked up at me, shock and disbelief in his eyes. "Only...." My voice caught, and I had to take a deep breath before I could go on. "Only let me stay. That's all I ask. Don't send me away."

"And then what, Eldon? Hide you away like some dark secret while she enjoys the prestige of being my wife?"

"I don't care about prestige. The only thing I care about is being with you in whatever capacity you'll have me."

It was pathetic, I knew, the depths I was willing to sink to just to keep some small piece of him, but my words made him smile—a bright, joyous smile that made his whole face light up. He stood up and took my hand, pulling me into his arms. "Don't you see? That's why you deserve it more than her."

He kissed me. He was so solid and so sure. I slid my hands inside his robe, sighing at the warmth of his smooth skin against my fingers. I could feel that power welling up in him, making his kisses harder and his touch insistent. It threatened to ignite a fire in both of us that would quickly make me forget my duties. But before it could sweep me away, we were interrupted by a knock at the door.

I was still trying to catch my breath when Xavier answered it.

It was a servant—a young boy I didn't know, who glanced with obvious curiosity between the prince in his robe and me. "Sire, the Lady Jessalyn sent me to find Cinder."

⊗

"Where were you?" Jessalyn snapped as I entered her room. "I've had the servants looking everywhere for you!"

Cinder

"He was with the prince," the servant volunteered. I resisted the urge to kick his feet from under him.

Jessalyn turned her disdainful gaze my way. "First you disgrace me at dinner, then you rush off to bother him before he even has breakfast." She turned away from me to regard herself in the mirror once more. She brushed powder over her nose. "I've seen the way you look at him. It's disgusting. I hate to think what he'll say if he ever finds out how you feel about him."

I turned away, not because I couldn't bear to face her, but because I didn't want her to see how her words made me smile. In the past, as recently as a day ago, her words would have stung, but not now. Instead, I thought of him. I thought of the way he'd held me. The way he'd touched me. I thought of the soft brush of his fingers against my cheeks, and the gentleness in his voice as he'd said, "She's not the one I love."

She could not hurt me. Whatever happened, my fate was no longer tied to hers. Maybe he'd marry her and maybe he wouldn't. Either way, I felt sure he'd allow me to stay.

Jessalyn was still talking. I was vaguely aware of her—not of her actual words, but of her tone—so petulant and disdainful. So arrogant.

I ignored her, and I called up in my mind the feel of him on top of me. The taste of him as he kissed me. The warmth of his mouth on the most intimate parts of me. I couldn't help but smile.

"Cinder, are you even listening?"

"Of course," I said. It was a lie, but it didn't matter.

She held her hairbrush out to me. "I'm having breakfast with him in half an hour," she said. "I need you to do my hair the way he likes."

I could have told her no. I could have walked away. But her shallow, self-centered venom couldn't touch me now. The memory of my night with him was like a still, quiet pool between Jessalyn and me. If she shouted, I might hear, but she couldn't touch me. She couldn't shatter the gentle joy he'd given me.

I brushed her hair, and she prattled on. She talked of the seamstress making the wedding gown, of which the ruffles were old-fashioned and unflattering. She talked of the servants, who all moved too slowly. She talked of the cake baker, who used too much cream in her frosting. She talked of the endless ways in which the world did not meet her exacting standards.

And through it all, I felt his touch on my skin.

Finally, she was ready to meet the prince. She left for breakfast, and I was sent to town to purchase a particular bath oil she simply couldn't live without.

I took my time. It was a gorgeous day. I felt light and free and somehow reborn. Part of me wanted to worry about what would happen next, but I chose to ignore it. I refused to let doubt darken my mood. For now, the memory of my night with him was enough. I wandered aimlessly through the market, smiling like a fool as I thought of him. I could still taste his kisses. I could smell him on my skin. It seemed like all I would ever need.

Eventually though, soft morning sunlight gave way to the bright, hot light of midday, and I admitted to myself I couldn't live in my memories forever. It was time to go back. It was almost lunchtime, and Jessalyn would undoubtedly be looking for me, ready to send me off on some brand new errand.

I knew something was wrong as soon as I returned. The halls of the palace seemed unusually hushed. Servants whispered together in corners. They glanced at me nervously as I passed.

As I neared Jessalyn's room, I heard shouting. When I rounded the corner, I found myself facing half a dozen guards. A couple seemed uncomfortable. Most were clearly amused. And in their midst was Jessalyn.

Her face was red. Her hands were balled into fists at her side. The hair I'd so carefully styled for her that morning was in disarray, hanging in a tangled mess down her back.

As soon as she saw me, she flew at me in a rage. "This is your fault!" she screamed. "You did this to me!"

The guard nearest me caught her before she reached me, grabbing her around the waist.

"Don't touch me!" she yelled, turning to pound his armored chest with her fists. He stood there, solid and unmoving, looking like he was having a hell of a time not bursting out laughing.

"My Lady," one of the others said, stepping forward. He had red braids on his shoulders, which I'd learned meant he was a captain. "Our orders are to escort you from the palace grounds."

"What?" I asked, stunned. "They're kicking us out?"

Nobody answered me. I wasn't sure they'd even heard me. They were too busy focusing on Jessalyn.

"You're leaving," the captain said to her, calm and rational. "It's that simple. The choice is yours: you can go peacefully, or you can make a scene. It matters little to us."

The one who'd kept her from attacking me laughed. "We'll haul you out kicking and screaming, if we have to."

She turned to glare at him. "You wouldn't dare!"

He grinned wickedly at her. "Try me."

I felt as if I'd been kicked in the stomach. After what had happened last night, Xavier was kicking us out? I couldn't believe it. I left Jessalyn to her fate and went in search of the man I loved.

The man who said he loved me back.

At his door, I found the same young servant who had interrupted us that very morning. He was sitting on the floor, leaning against Xavier's door, but as soon as he saw me, he scrambled to his feet.

"He told me to wait here for you, sir," he said. He pulled a piece of paper from his pocket and held it out to me. "He said to make sure you got this."

The note was short. It said only:

>*There's something I must do. I'll be back in three days. Trust me.*
>
>*Love — X*

Nothing else.

I turned the paper over, stupidly hoping to find more on the back, but there was nothing there.

"I don't understand," I said, more to myself than to the young servant. "Where did he go? Why are they kicking us out?"

The boy shook his head. "Not you, sir," he said. "Only the lady."

"Not me?"

He shook his head again. "Everybody's talking about it, sir. They say he specifically said not to let the lady take you."

"Who's everybody?"

"The servants, sir." He grinned at me. "We hear lots, you know."

Of course I knew. I was one.

"And what about the wedding?" It was scheduled to take place in only three days.

"It's still on, sir. They say he specifically told them he'd be back in time."

The wedding was still on, and yet Jessalyn was being kicked out? "Stop calling me sir," I said.

"Yes, sir."

I sighed. I had a renewed sympathy for Xavier. "Where did he go?"

"Nobody knows for sure, sir, but the rumor is, he went back."

"Back where?"

"Back to your town," he said. "Back to where you're

from."

If that was true, time was short. The trip from my home had taken us two days, although we'd been moving at the speed of the carriage. Alone on horseback, it was possible he could make it there and back in time for the wedding, but there'd be little time to spare. "Why is he going there?"

"They say he picked the wrong girl."

The wrong girl?

"They say the prince meant to pick her twin, but Jessalyn locked her sister in the closet and tricked the prince into taking her instead."

It was absurd. After all, I knew Penelope wasn't the right girl any more than Jess was. I also knew Jess hadn't done anything as drastic as locking her sister in the closet. On the other hand, I sure wouldn't have put it past her if it had come to that.

Was it was possible Xavier had decided to go through with the marriage, but had decided Penelope was the better choice? She was, after all, not nearly so conniving. If I had to see him wed to one of my marriageable cousins, I certainly would have chosen Penelope over Jess.

Still, it made no sense.

"Is there anything else?" I asked.

The boy grinned at me and leaned closer as if sharing a remarkable secret. "Only that nobody's too sorry to see her go." He straightened back up and made a noticeable effort to stop smiling. It didn't quite work. "That's all," he said. "Sir."

The next few days were the strangest of my life. For the first time in years, nobody was giving me orders. I had no duties. No chores. I had absolutely nothing to do.

Jessalyn was gone. The rumors said she had indeed been carried kicking and screaming out of the palace. The guards deposited her just outside the gate. They say she stayed there for several hours, yelling and pleading and doing her best to convince anybody who would listen that it was all a horrible mistake. Eventually, the guards tired of jeering at her. They resorted to pelting her with dirt clods. When those ran out, they threatened horse dung. After that, she gave up and wandered away. She was never heard from again.

I didn't miss her.

I quickly found idleness didn't suit me, and of course there was plenty of work to be done. The palace was bordering on chaos. There was still a wedding to be planned, albeit with no bride and no groom. Xavier's mother took over, and preparations resumed in earnest. Nobody knew what to do about the bride's dress, but other than that, things were much as they had been before, except without Jessalyn's constant complaints.

The eve of Xavier's birthday dawned warm and bright and beautiful. It was the day of the wedding. The ceremony was planned for late in the evening, due to some ancient custom I knew nothing about. A feast was to be served after. The servants were busy, but not too busy to gossip.

The prince was home. Or maybe he wasn't. He'd brought a bride. Or maybe he hadn't. It all depended on who you asked. Some said he'd rescued a princess from a tower, but whether he'd done so by climbing her hair or by defeating a dragon or both was up for debate. I followed the gossip obsessively for the first few hours, desperate for word of Xavier, but eventually I realized it was pointless. Xavier would return home at some point, with or without a bride. I would learn the truth of it all eventually. Worrying about it now would only drive me insane.

After that, I bent my head to my work and did my best to ignore the gossip.

The day passed in a frantic blur of activity. When sunset came, I was in the dining room, helping set the many tables.

Cinder

"Eldon Cinder!"

The voice rang through the dining room like a bell. Complete silence fell as everybody turned toward the door. It was one of the guards. "Is Eldon Cinder here?" he asked again.

Everybody turned my way. I cleared my throat and made myself speak. "I'm Eldon."

"You're to come with me."

He didn't wait to see if I was following. He simply turned and strode purposefully away. I had to hurry to catch up.

"Where are we going?" I asked as I jogged along behind him through the palace corridor.

"To the wedding."

"Has the prince returned?"

"He has. Not more than five minutes ago. Went straight to the wedding in his riding clothes."

"Am I in some kind of trouble?"

"I don't know."

"But what—"

He stopped dead in his tracks, turning to face me. It happened so fast, I almost ran into him. "I don't know, sir. The prince told me to bring you. So I am. That's all."

Off he went again, and I rushed to keep up—right to the door of the cavernous palace courtroom.

I stopped there in the entry, looking up the aisle. Guests were seated on each side, dressed in their finest garb. I was suddenly horribly aware of my own clothes, faded and patched and dirty from the work I'd done through the day.

On the dais at the head of the room stood a flock of confused clerks, their long dark robes matching their long beards and dour expressions. The disapproval on their faces was evident. Next to them stood Xavier's parents, the king and queen. The king was baffled. The queen seemed intrigued. And in front of them all was Xavier, wearing the broadest smile I'd ever seen.

"Eldon!" Xavier called when he saw me. The room was so big, he practically had to yell. "Where were you?"

Everybody turned in their seats to stare at me, and I felt myself blush. "I was folding napkins."

Xavier laughed. The audience buzzed.

"Well," the prince said, "are you going to come up here, or will you make me wait all night?"

Walking up the aisle was the hardest thing I've ever done. My knees shook. My palms were damp. On each side of me there were faces, wide eyes staring at me as I passed. There were hushed whispers and people straining to see me past those who were seated along the aisle.

And then, finally there in front of me, was Xavier, as handsome and regal as ever, even in his rumpled riding clothes.

"Xav—Excellency?"

He smiled at my near-blunder, but all he said was, "Take off your shoe."

Behind me, a wave of whispers ran through the crowd, along with a few nervous chuckles.

"My shoe?" I asked stupidly.

"Yes," he said. "The right one."

I used my left foot to toe my worn right boot off. Xavier reached into the pocket of his velvet jacket and pulled out....

The shoe.

It bore little resemblance to the lacy, delicate sandal I'd worn to the ball. Milton had drooled on it a good deal over the past few days, and Xavier had clearly had to squish it to get it into his pocket.

He held it out to me. "Put it on."

Was this some kind of joke? "It won't fit."

"I think it will."

"I'm telling you, it won't. My foot is too big."

He leaned forward to whisper in my ear. "You're not the

Cinder

only one who leaves gifts for the witch."

Of course. The witch.

I found myself smiling. The rumors had been true—he had gone back. But not to get Penelope.

"What did you give her?"

He grinned at me. "A whole box of mice." I couldn't tell if he was serious or not. He knelt in front of me and held the shoe for me to slip on.

I still didn't know exactly what was going on. The whole thing seemed crazy. But he was the prince. More than that, he was the man I loved, and he was on his knees in front of me, in front of his parents, in front of a court full of people, waiting for me to trust him.

I slipped my toes in. That should have been as much as I could manage. The ball of my foot shouldn't have gone past the straps.

But it did.

Somehow, my foot slipped inside. It wasn't that the shoe fit my foot. It was that suddenly, my foot fit the shoe. As Xavier stood up, watching me expectantly, I realized why he'd gone back to see the witch.

There, in front of everybody, amidst startled gasps and gaping mouths, the magic took hold. The tingling warmth of it spread up from my foot, over my ankles, up my thighs. I felt the changes again as they happened—hips widening, shoulders narrowing, hair growing, the structure of my face changing. One minute I was wearing my tattered clothes, a worn boot on one foot and a ridiculously ornate slipper that by all rights was way too small on the other, and the next moment I wore a woman's dress. It was long and white, tight and binding around my rib cage and breasts, billowing around my hips, full and heavy around my legs. On my feet, I still wore one boot and one lady's shoe, but they were hidden by the fullness of the skirt, and the magic somehow kept me from hobbling gracelessly on the uneven heels.

The crowd seemed to gasp as one, and then, there was utter silence.

I met Xavier's smiling eyes. "There's the girl I've been looking for," he said.

He held his hand out to me.

I wanted to take it, and yet, I wanted to know what this new magic entailed. Was I to remain like this? I hadn't wanted to be a woman to begin with. I certainly didn't want it to become a regular occurrence.

He must have seen the hesitation on my face, because he smiled. "Trust me."

Outside, the clock began to chime.

"You're almost out of time," the king said.

I took Xavier's hand

His smile grew, and he turned to the clerk. "We're ready." The clock chimed again, and he added, "Make it fast."

The clerk's shocked expression might have made me laugh if I hadn't been so worried about hyperventilating from nerves. The only thing that kept me together was Xavier—the strength of his hand holding mine. The sheer joy I saw shining in his eyes as he looked at me. The surety that this was what he wanted.

The ceremony was a blur. I must have said, "I do." The clock continued its slow, melodic chime. And then the clerk declared, "You now are joined as man and umm...wife?" He cleared his throat nervously. "You may kiss your bride."

And just as the twelfth chime rang out, Xavier kissed me. It wasn't romantic. It wasn't passionate. It was nothing more than a chaste, quick touch against my lips.

That worried me, but his eyes begged me to trust him. He squeezed my hand, assuring me it would be fine.

The spectators cheered, but Xavier turned toward them, holding up his hands to call for silence. They quieted quickly, and Xavier turned to his father.

"You agree I've met the requirement?" he asked. "I've

taken a wife before my birthday?"

His father looked startled, but he nodded. "You have."

Xavier turned to the clerk. "Declare me heir to the kingdom."

There was a hustle of robed clerks, and a circlet was brought forward. It took forever. I stood there, my knees shaking, my heart in my throat, wondering what would happen next. There were speeches, and Xavier swore oath after oath. Finally, with much ceremony and overly-wordy oration, just as the clock struck one, the circlet was placed upon his brow, and he was declared Heir Confirmed to His Majesty's Kingdom, Crown Prince of the Land.

This time, there was no cheering. The crowd seemed to be waiting for him to make a speech.

"The law says I must take a wife before my birthday," he declared, his voice strong and pitched to carry to the far corners of the chamber, "but it doesn't say I must keep her."

Another ripple went through the crowd, the buzz of confusion and whispered questions. My heart sank. My mouth went dry. Was this it? He had secured his title and his inheritance, and now he would reject me?

He turned to me and said, "Eldon, take off the shoe."

I did, and the spell fall away. It felt like dropping a heavy wool cloak from my shoulders. I half expected to see some remnant of it puddled on the floor around my feet—one of which was now bare. I looked up to find Xavier smiling at me. "And there's the boy I fell in love with."

"Son," the king said quietly, "I'm not sure this entirely appropriate."

Xavier smiled at me. "Appropriate is boring."

This time, he kissed me the right way, deep and sweet and passionate. There was more cheering, and a celebration that spread throughout the land and lasted a fortnight. And so it was that Augustus Alexandre Kornelius Xavier Redmond became the Crown Prince, and I became both his husband and his wife. More importantly, I remained forevermore his partner, and his friend. He swept me away to his castle where we had fish for dinner once a week, and champagne that tasted like sunlight, and Milton never tired of playing fetch with that silly old shoe.

And the three of us lived—
Well....
I'm sure you can guess how it ends.

The End

About the Author

Marie Sexton lives in Colorado. She's a fan of just about anything that involves muscular young men piling on top of each other. In particular, she loves the Denver Broncos and enjoys going to the games with her husband. Her imaginary friends often tag along. Marie has one daughter, two cats, and one dog, all of whom seem bent on destroying what remains of her sanity. She loves them anyway.

Website and Blog:
http://mariesexton.net/

Facebook:
http://www.facebook.com/MarieSexton.author/

Twitter:
https://twitter.com/MarieSexton

Email:
msexton.author@gmail.com

If you enjoyed Cinder, you might also enjoy

Song of Oestend
by Marie Sexton

Turn the page for a preview.

CHAPTER ONE

Aren had heard of the wraiths, of course. Everyone had.

The thing was, nobody believed the stories were real. Not where he came from, anyway.

But on his first night in the town of Milton, as the wind howled outside and beat against the shuttered windows of his room, Aren Montrell lay awake and trembling in his bed. He began to remember every story he'd ever heard about the wraiths.

Every nanny—and probably every parent, too, although Aren wouldn't know about that—told stories of children found cold and lifeless in the morning because some spiteful adult had left the window open after tucking the kids into bed. It was said that wraiths came on the darkest of nights, stealing the breath from any person fool enough not to be inside, behind closed doors. Even back home, across the sea, in the bustling cities of Lanstead, many houses had signs of protection over their front doors. Still, Aren had never had reason to believe the stories were true. He'd always believed the signs were more decorative than anything. But he'd quickly discovered upon his arrival in Oestend that every building had the signs, not just over the front door, but over every door, and the windows as well. Even the barn where weary travellers boarded their horses had been warded against the wraiths.

He'd seen the way the hostel-keeper and his wife had

systematically checked each and every window in each and every room. He'd made note of the double bars on both the front and back doors. Then, as he was finishing his dinner, the wife had stopped next to him. Her hand on his shoulder was rough and calloused and her face was grim. "Don't open your window once the generator goes on," she'd said. "I don't care how hot you get."

Aren wasn't even sure what she meant by the word 'generator', but she'd moved on then, before Aren could ask questions. He'd nearly jumped out of his skin when the generator had kicked on a few minutes later—not that he would have known that was what it was if the woman hadn't warned him. It made a nagging, low-pitched drone that Aren didn't so much hear as feel, low in the base of his skull. He found it nerve-racking, but it was obvious the locals were used to it. He'd gone to his room feeling less than confident.

Maybe this had been a mistake. Maybe he shouldn't have come here, to the pitiful, dusty edge of the world. But after the incident at the university, running to Oestend had seemed so logical. So obvious. A suddenly sympathetic Professor Sheldon had helped Aren secure a job at one of the large ranches on the Oestend prairie. At the time, Aren had thought Sheldon had done it out of pity. Now, as he faced the realisation that this was a life he did not know how to live, Aren began to also realise he'd been duped. No doubt Sheldon and Professor Dean Birmingham, the man Aren had thought of as his lover for the past four years, were laughing together over their brandy, pleased they'd manage to rid themselves of him.

"Fuck you," Aren said. His voice was loud in the small room. He sounded strong, and it gave him courage. "Fuck you!" he said again, louder this time, feeling more sure of himself. "I'm not scared."

He jumped as somebody pounded on the wall of his room. Not one of the wraiths that may or may not have been outside in the wind. It came from the room next to Aren's. "People trying to sleep in here!" the man on the other side of the wall yelled.

Aren couldn't believe anybody could sleep through the buzz of the generator and the racket of the wind and yet be kept awake by somebody talking, but he didn't want to cause trouble, so he resolved to stop cussing at people who were halfway across the world. Still, his outburst had given him the strength he needed to examine his situation rationally.

There was no point in being scared. If there really were wraiths in Oestend, it was obvious the locals knew how to handle them. The man who'd hired him had directed him to this particular hostel for the night. Presumably he wouldn't have sent Aren to a place that was known for allowing its tenants to be killed in their sleep. Although the shutters on windows rattled, they seemed solid enough, and Aren would have bet his last coin there was a warding sign over the window as well. He had to trust those things would be enough to keep him safe.

He pulled the blanket over his head and snuggled down under the covers. At least the bed was soft and the sheets were clean. Tomorrow, a man from the ranch would arrive to take him to his new home. Whatever this backwater land wanted to throw at him, Aren was sure he was ready.

He was right on most counts. He was ready for the dust. He was ready for the wind. He was ready for the two-day trip to the ranch.

What he wasn't ready for was Deacon.

Deacon was the man who arrived to take Aren to the BarChi Ranch. Deacon had come into town the night before, but had apparently elected to spend the night elsewhere—in the stables or at the whorehouse or at another inn, Aren didn't know, and didn't care. Deacon arrived at the hostel the next morning driving a wooden wagon drawn by a pair of sturdy draught horses.

The first thing Aren noticed about him was the deep colour of his skin. Back on the continent, skin-tones ran from white to pink to golden, but one rarely saw anybody darker than the sun could make them. Deacon, on the other hand, had skin that was a rich, dark reddish-brown. He wore a straw cowboy hat, and his pitch-black hair hung in a queue down his back. Aren supposed him to be around thirty years old. He was tall and broad and muscular and rough and everything Aren might have expected from a man who'd spent his entire life doing hard labour on a remote Oestend ranch. He was exactly the kind of man who usually managed to make Aren feel small and insignificant simply by being there. He looked at Aren's pile of luggage with barely disguised amusement.

"You got an awful lot of stuff," he said, turning his mocking gaze onto Aren. "What's in all those?"

Deacon's scrutiny made him uncomfortable. Aren tried to smooth his light brown hair down—it had grown out longer than he'd ever had it, which was still short by Oestend standards. It was too short to pull into a queue like Deacon's, and though Aren tried to keep it straight, it seemed determined to form soft curls around his ears. He had a hard enough time getting men to take him seriously because of his small stature. Having hair that curled like a girl's wasn't going to help.

"Well?" Deacon asked, still waiting for an answer. "What's in the bags?"

Aren forced himself to stop fidgeting, although he couldn't quite meet Deacon's eyes. "My clothes. Books. Art supplies."

"Art supplies?" Deacon asked, as if the words held no meaning for him.

"Yes," Aren said, and for some reason, Deacon's absurd

question gave him the strength he needed to stand up straight and face the rough cowboy in front of him. "Canvas and paint."

Deacon's eyebrows went up, and although he didn't laugh, it was clear he wanted to. "Good thing. Barn's needed a new coat of paint for a while now."

Aren felt his cheeks turning red, and he hid it by turning to pick up the nearest suitcase. It had seemed perfectly reasonable to bring his art supplies with him, especially since he feared both paint and canvas might be hard to come by on the ranch. It bothered him that Deacon had managed to make him feel foolish for it. The fact that he'd done it within moments of meeting him only made it sting more.

One by one, he loaded his many suitcases into the wagon. He could feel Deacon's gaze upon him the entire time. He moved quickly because he knew they had other things to do in town before they left. When his last bag was in the wagon, he turned to face Deacon again, ready for the mockery he'd seen in Deacon's eyes before. He was surprised to see Deacon was no longer laughing at him. He was watching him appraisingly, and Aren thought he even saw a hint of approval in his dark eyes.

"Would have done that for you, you know," he said.

Then why didn't you? Of course, if he'd wanted help, he could have asked, but this was obviously a world where physical strength earned more respect than education or refinement. Aren hated to give other men a reason to think he was weak. Just because he wasn't made of muscle like Deacon didn't mean he couldn't handle his own luggage. A familiar feeling of angry rebellion bloomed in Aren's chest. "I'm not helpless," he snapped.

Deacon's look of puzzled amusement returned. He shook his head. "Why're you mad?" he asked.

It was a good question. Why was he mad? Because Deacon was laughing at him? Because he hadn't helped with the bags? Or because he seemed surprised that Aren hadn't asked for help with them? Or was it only because here, just as at the university, he was bound to be seen as less than a man by all the other men around him?

"I'm just tired," Aren said, which wasn't exactly a lie. He'd been travelling for more than a month to reach this point—four weeks on the small, stinky ship from Lanstead to Francshire, Oestend's eastern port, being seasick most of the way, followed by two nights straight on the noisy, rickety train from Francshire to Milton, the western-most point of what could loosely be termed 'civilisation' in Oestend. Although he'd managed to get a few hours of sleep at the hostel the night before, he still felt terribly out of sorts. "I feel I've barely slept in ages."

The smile that spread across Deacon's face this time wasn't mocking. It was friendly, and a little bit mischievous. "Don't worry. Pretty sure you'll sleep good tonight."

"Why is that?" Aren asked.

"Staying at the McAllen farm," Deacon said. "Lots of maids and daughters there." He winked at Aren. "One of them's bound to tuck you in."

Aren hoped the sinking feeling those words caused wasn't apparent on his face. He fought to keep his voice steady. "I see."

"We best get moving if we want to get there before the wraiths get us."

"Of course," Aren said, although at that moment, he would have preferred to take his chances with the wraiths.

They made a few quick stops for supplies before heading out into the prairie. Aren hadn't seen much of Milton when he'd arrived. The hostel he'd stayed at was near the outskirts of the east side. They had to drive west all the way through town before leaving.

Although the cities back in Lanstead had their slums too, the parts Aren had been familiar with were filled with upscale shops and brightly-painted town homes. Stained glass windows had recently become a fad, and nearly every home sported at least one, usually as prominent and garish as it could be. Glancing around the dusty town of Milton, Aren saw nothing of the sort. The walkways fronting the businesses were bare wooden planks. The buildings he saw looked as if they'd never seen a single coat of paint. The few painted signs he saw were faded to the point of being practically useless.

"Some of these buildings don't even have windows," Aren said.

Deacon shrugged. "Glass is expensive. Plus, it's damn hard to patch the hole in the wall if it breaks."

Everywhere he looked, it seemed Aren saw no colour at all—only varying shades of brown and grey. He found it a bit depressing.

In the town's centre lay a large wooden platform. It almost looked like a stage. Aren might have thought it was for executions, except there was no sign of a gallows.

"What's that for?" he asked Deacon.

Deacon's jaw clenched, as if the question angered him. He didn't look at Aren. "That's where they used to sell the slaves."

"Slaves?" Aren asked, alarmed. "They still have slavery here?"

"Not anymore," Deacon said, "but it lasted longer than you'd probably think."

Once they'd passed the last building, Deacon drove onto a rutted trail that led into the long, golden-green grass of the Oestend prairie. They were headed due west, presumably towards the BarChi Ranch, where Aren had managed to secure a job as a bookkeeper. As the bustle of the town fell behind them, Aren found himself feeling simultaneously liberated and scared to death. In leaving Milton, he was abandoning all vestiges of the civilised society he'd grown up in. Ahead of him, Oestend held only ranches, mines, buffalo, and mile after mile of prairie. He was leaving behind the trappings of luxury. Back home in Lanstead, most homes had running water. A few even had electricity. He would find none of that here in Oestend.

Lanstead had first colonised Oestend a hundred and fifty years earlier, but shipping goods back and forth had proved to be more trouble and more expense than it was worth. Since that time, the empire had long since lost interest in the remote land, and the colonies had become more or less independent. The eastern seaboard was where the majority of the population resided, living off what the sea provided. Further inland, most of Oestend's limited prosperity came from the many mines to the south and fur and fishing in the north. Of course, everybody in Oestend, from miners and trappers to the inn-keepers and blacksmiths, had to eat, and that was where the ranches came in. By accepting a position at one of them, Aren had committed himself to a life that was considered downright primitive by most of his colleagues.

Ex-colleagues, he reminded himself. It was time he stopped thinking of himself as a bourgeois university student from the most cosmopolitan city on the continent. He was now a bookkeeper for an Oestend rancher.

"You work for Jeremiah?" Aren asked Deacon.

Deacon frowned at the question. "Guess so."

"Are you his son?"

"Nope."

"Are you the foreman?"

Deacon tipped his head a bit to the side, squinting as if the question confused him. "Guess I'm the closest thing we got." He glanced over at Aren, looking him up and down in an appraising way—though not as if he were interested in Aren sexually. Aren thought it was probably closer to the way he might have examined a cow he was taking to market.

"You're not married, are you?" Deacon asked.

It seemed like such a strange question, completely out of nowhere, and it surprised Aren. "No," he said. "Why?"

"Possible Fred McAllen'll be throwing one of his daughters at you tonight."

Aren found that alarming. It was bad enough he might have to face women who wanted sex, but if his host was expecting it for some reason, things were going to be even more uncomfortable than he'd imagined. "You mean he encourages his daughters to 'tuck in' the guests?"

Deacon laughed. "Hell, no! He catches one of them doing that, he might take a shotgun to you."

That was something of a relief. "Then what—?"

"I mean a bride."

Any fleeting sense of relief Aren had felt disappeared. "A what?"

"The McAllens have a lot of daughters, and not many eligible sons around here to marry them off to."

"I'm not getting married!"

Deacon laughed. "No, not tonight you ain't. I'm just saying, they'll likely be sizing you up as a possible husband."

"Holy Saints, that's the last thing I need."

"It's possible they'll hold off. Wait to see if you pan out before letting one of their girls marry you."

"Is there anything I can do to discourage them?"

Deacon laughed, and somehow the look he turned on Aren seemed far more congenial than it had been before. "Make yourself look like bad husband material, I guess."

"How do I do that?"

"I don't know. Never thought about it before. I suppose act stupid. Or mean."

Nobody in the world would believe Aren if he tried to act mean. Stupid, though? Stupid he thought he could do.

CHAPTER TWO

A couple of hours before sunset they rode over a ridge and the McAllen farm appeared below them. There was a house, a barn, and a few small outbuildings. Lined up behind the barn were pen after pen of pigs. Rising high above it all, casting its long shadow over the house, was the biggest windmill Aren had ever seen. It was also the strangest. It obviously wasn't part of any mill. Its base ended in a giant contraption that looked like an engine that had fallen off a passing train.

"What is that?" Aren asked.

Deacon laughed. "Ain't you ever seen a windmill before?"

"Not one like that."

"Runs the generators," Deacon said. "That transformer at the bottom stores the energy so we still have juice even if the wind stops. Not that it does that too often out here."

"There weren't any windmills in town."

"Generators run on different things. Most people in town use coal. These will burn coal too, if they need to, but hauling wagonloads of it out into the prairie ain't exactly efficient."

They were getting closer to the farm. Aren could hear the pigs now, and even worse, he could smell them. The stench was horrendous.

"Hog farm," Deacon said when he saw Aren covering his nose with the sleeve of his shirt. "Good news is, no hogs on the BarChi. Cows and horses shit too, but somehow, it don't smell near as bad."

"Thank the Saints for small favours," Aren mumbled.

They were greeted outside the barn by six young women. Four of them wore rough-spun trousers and blouses, and Aren noticed all four of them had opened the top few buttons of their shirts. Their necks were tanned, but the soft swells of flesh below their temptingly gaping necklines were pale and creamy, and the girls seemed completely unashamed as they jockeyed for the best position to display them to Deacon.

The other two girls stood apart. They wore ankle-length dresses covered by long white aprons and had lace kerchiefs over their neatly-braided hair. And every single button was done up tightly. They ignored Deacon and came straight to Aren.

"Hello," the taller one said to him, shaking his hand. "I'm Beth. This is my sister, Alissa. We're so pleased you're here."

Aren felt himself blushing. He could have sworn his throat was closing up, blocking off any words he might wish to speak. He'd spent most of his life in all-male boarding schools, and the rest of it at the all-male university. The only woman he'd ever known at all had been his nanny, but that had been twenty years before, when he was only a child. He'd avoided the society parties his father had thrown and had never gone to the red-light district with his classmates. Whether they were whores or maids or true ladies didn't matter—Aren had no idea how to behave around women. He looked over at Deacon, hoping for some help, but Deacon was lost amongst giggling maids.

"You'll join us at the house for dinner, I hope?" Beth asked. She had golden hair and blue eyes, and Aren supposed she was pretty.

"Ummm..." He looked to Deacon again but couldn't even manage to meet his eyes. Beth followed the direction of his gaze and seemed to think she understood his thoughts.

"Don't worry," she said. "The maids will make sure he gets dinner in the barn."

Next to her, Alissa snorted. "Dinner—plus dessert, I'm sure."

Beth glared at her. "Alissa, don't be crude."

Alissa blushed deep red and ducked her head. She was shorter than her sister and skinnier, with none of her sister's alluring curves. Her hair was darker than Beth's, and she had freckles across her long nose. She glanced sideways at Beth, then glared with open hostility at the maids surrounding Deacon.

Poor Alissa, Aren found himself thinking. Lost in her sister's shadow when potential suitors arrived, held hostage by the rules of her class, not allowed to unhook her top button and try for Deacon's attention either.

"Come on," Beth said to him, turning towards the house, obviously expecting him to follow. "I'll show you to the guest room."

"What about Deacon?" Aren asked. He knew it was foolish, but he wasn't about to let himself be led like a lamb to slaughter by Beth and Alissa. "Shouldn't you show him to his room, too?"

Beth seemed at a loss for words, but Alissa wasn't. "He sleeps in the barn," she said.

The rigidity of the social structure was starting to become clear. Back in Lanstead, society was also stratified by position and income, but for some reason, he hadn't expected to find the same type of issues here in Oestend.

"I'll sleep with Deacon in the barn," he said, then felt himself blush when he realised how that might sound.

"Don't be silly," Beth said. "We have a bed for you at the house."

"W—well..." he stammered, unsure what to say. He was saved by Deacon, who walked up behind him and clapped him on the back.

"Listen, ladies," he said, and he seemed to include all six women in that statement, "Aren and I have to get these horses unhitched and brushed and fed, and there's not much daylight left. If you'll just bring us a bite to eat, we'll be happy enough."

It was obvious the maids were thrilled and the daughters less so, but they all left, and Aren did his best to help Deacon unhook the team, although he felt he probably got in the way more than anything. Eventually, Deacon handed him a brush and pointed him towards one of the horses. The beast stared at him with black eyes, its ears back, and Aren could have sworn it was daring him to step within kicking range.

"I don't know how," he said to Deacon.

The big cowboy rolled his eyes. "You never used a brush before?"

"Not on a horse."

"Not much to it," Deacon said. "Just go in the direction of the hair."

Aren wasn't exactly reassured. He was afraid the big mare would suddenly decide she didn't want to be tended to after all, but he didn't want to look too craven in front of Deacon, so he slowly approached the horse and started to brush. Deacon was in the next stall, brushing down the other horse. He'd taken his hat off, and one of the maids had obviously undone his queue while flirting with him, because his thick, black hair hung loose down his back.

"Can I ask a question without you laughing at me?" Aren asked.

"Probably not." But his tone was friendly, so Aren asked

anyway.

"The wraiths are real?"

Deacon didn't seem surprised by the question. "Yup. They're real. You boys from the continent never believe the stories, but you wander out after dark, you'll find out they're true right quick."

"They only come when there's no moon?"

Deacon laughed. "That's another story you boys always have in your heads." He shook his head. "If it's dark, the wraiths can come. Only a fool relies on the moon to protect him."

"But we're safe as long as we're indoors?"

"Might be safe enough if everything's locked down tight, but the only way to be sure is to be inside the net."

"What net?"

"You seen the wards, right? Over the doors and windows?"

"Yes."

"Used to be the wards was enough. But over the years, they stopped working. Don't ask why," he said, glancing at Aren. Aren snapped his mouth shut on the words, which had already been halfway out of his mouth. "Nobody rightly knows. But then along came a man figured out how to fix it."

"By making a generator?"

"Exactly. The generator connects them all. Makes a net the wraiths can't get through."

"Like a fishing net?"

"Well, you can't actually see the damn thing, but I guess it's the same idea."

"So as long as the generator's on, it's safe to walk outside between the buildings?"

"Wouldn't recommend it," Deacon said. "They say wraiths can get through the net if they want to. They just don't like it. Long as we're all indoors, they got no reason to bother. But you go walking around in the dark, they may just decide it's worth a try."

"What do the wraiths look like?"

"Can't really say. Never seen one. If you watch out a window, you can't see much. Things blowing around in the wind, dust devils. Some people think they're in the wind. Some people say they're invisible." He shrugged. "I only know they're there. Seen enough people they've killed to know it ain't a story."

"How do they kill you?"

"Can't really say that, either. Never any blood or wounds. Bodies are blue, like they suffocated, or froze to death."

"What about animals?"

"What about them?"

"How do you keep the cattle safe? Do you have to bring them all in each night?"

"Wraiths only kill people."

"Why?"

"Saints, I don't know!" Deacon said, although there was something in his voice that made Aren wonder if he was telling him the truth. "That's just the way it is."

By Marie Sexton:

Promises
A to Z
The Letter Z
Strawberries for Dessert
Paris A to Z
Fear, Hope, and Bread Pudding
Between Sinners and Saints
Song of Oestend
Saviours of Oestend
Blind Space
Second Hand
Never a Hero
Family Man
Flowers for Him
One More Soldier
Normal Enough
Roped In
Chapter 5 and the Axe-Wielding Maniac
Apartment 14 and the Devil Next Door
Lost Along the Way
Shotgun
Winter Oranges
Trailer Trash
Damned If You Do
Making Waves
The Well
One Man's Trash
Terms of Service

Praise for Marie Sexton's

Song of Oestend

1st Place for Best Gay Fantasy in the 2011 Rainbow Awards

"Symbols have power, which Aren and Deacon prove when death threatens to separate them, but those symbols are made even more powerful when constructed in love. Though the journey isn't always easy, though it takes some time for Aren and Deacon to find the crossroads that will alter the paths their lives have been on, it was so well worth the trip."

-- *Top 2 Bottom Reviews*

"Song of Oestend is another fantastic offering from one of the best writers in this genre."

-- *Bittersweet Reviews*

Praise for Marie Sexton's

Never a Hero

"If you're all about the character-driven romance? Oh yeah, Never a Hero is the book for you."

-- The Allure of Books

"The story was brilliantly written, creating a world of sensitivity and reality through the psyche of both Nick and Owen." –

- The Jeep Diva

"The writing is great, as you can pretty much count on with Marie Sexton. I fell in love right along with Owen and Nick. And while this is book 5 in the Tucker Springs series, it works 100% as a standalone. I would definitely recommend this one to m/m romance readers!"

-- Red Hot Books

Praise for Marie Sexton's

Between Sinners and Saints

"I absolutely loved this book and highly recommend it."

-- *Reviews by Jessewave*

"I would strongly recommend Between Sinners and Saints to any fan of the M/M genre and will be reading this story again in the future."

-- *Literary Nymphs Reviews*

"This was an emotional book about trust, love and true devotion. The love scenes were sweet and sensuous and I couldn't get enough of them."

— *Dark Divas Reviews*

Printed in Great Britain
by Amazon